THE AMISH
SCHOOLTEACHER

THE AMISH SCHOOLTEACHER

A ROMANCE

JERRY EICHER

Good Books

New York, New York

CHAPTER 1

THE WHINE OF THE GREYHOUND BUS FILLED MARY WAGLER'S EARS AS SHE shifted on the seat and pressed her bonnet against the dusty window glass for the umpteenth time. The small town of West Union was only a short distance ahead. They had been winding west on Highway 125 through southern Ohio for what seemed like hours. The Ohio River lay a mile or so to the south. Mary had studied the state map before leaving her small Amish community located in central Ohio. She wasn't traveling that far from home, and yet this was her first time to venture abroad alone. Her destination was a sister Amish community, to serve as their schoolteacher. She wasn't in rebellion or running away. She wasn't nervous, or jittery, which would have been perfectly normal, considering.

This venture was a relief, in fact, a fresh start on her own, without the stifling shadow of her three older sisters. Esther, Lois, and Phoebe were married and settled down, but that hadn't kept them from visiting the Belle Center Amish schoolhouse last year to see how she was doing. That might have been nice in a sisterly sort of way, except they really were there to drop advice from their own teaching years. Each of her sisters had been beloved schoolteachers in their time, and had snagged husbands before two teaching terms had passed.

This was Mary's second term and no husband was in sight. "Keep the story hour after lunch short," Esther had advised.

"You don't want the students falling asleep and word getting around the community. You know what I mean . . . school-teacher can't keep her own students interested."

Mary had smiled and nodded, but she ignored Esther's advice. Everyone knew that she read stories well and could keep a child enthralled for hours while they listened to her animated voice. She was the first one her nieces ran to at the family gatherings, to hop up on her knee, a book in their hands. She loved children, and had experienced two successful terms. Hadn't the school board asked her back for another year, even if there was no husband on the horizon? Edwin Mast had asked her again for a date, his third request, along with two other men earlier, but none of them interested Mary. If she allowed her sisters to have their way, she'd already be married to one of those men, probably with a child on the way.

"You should take him," Phoebe had said of Edwin when she heard the news from Mam. "That is, if he asks again." As if there was any doubt.

"His family is excellent." Lois had joined forces with Phoebe. "His mother also taught school."

So maybe Mary *was* running? But not in a bad way. In a good way. Right into the life she wanted. What that was, she wasn't sure, but it didn't include any man she knew, or sisters who breathed advice down her neck. Not that she was opposed to marriage. There just hadn't been a man who properly impressed her yet. She doubted if any such man would pop up in this new community. At least she wasn't getting her hopes high. No use setting herself up for disappointment. Plus, she had other things to think about, like new students, a new home, a whole new life away from her closest friends and family.

Mam at least seemed to understand. "Did you pray about this?" was the only question she had asked.

"Of course," Mary had replied, and had shown Mam the letter the Adams County school board had written after she had responded to their advertisement published in the Amish weekly newspaper, *The Budget.*

The ad had read, "Schoolteacher needed in Adams County. Should have some experience. Room and board provided. Wages, the usual."

"Dear Mary," the Adams County school board letter had written. "We were quite happy to receive your résumé in the mail, and wrote letters to the school board members in your home district. Also to your bishop, Henry Byler. They had nothing but good things to say about your time teaching school in the Belle Center Amish community the last two years. Their only regret is that you did not accept their offer of another term. We would be honored to have you teach at our school district in Adams County."

The names had been signed at the end of the letter. Names she didn't know, but now she was riding on the bus to meet the people they belonged to. Not that she expected the whole school board to greet her in West Union, but no doubt several of their wives would be there to transport her to the boarding house, as was customary.

She would stay with an older couple, Leon and Lavina Hochstetler, who lived within walking distance of the schoolhouse. She knew that much from the details in the follow-up letter from the Adams County school board.

The bus whined, slowing again, but the sign outside the window read Lynx, not West Union. Mary sighed and leaned back. She had to relax. This new world would arrive in the Lord's timing. She had only to pray and believe in His leading that a new life lay before her. A life which would include everything right and good, and in the Lord's will.

Marcus Yoder drove his horse, Rowdy, across the rattling covered bridge on his way to the bus station in West Union. He was fifteen minutes early and consequently several of the evening chores awaited him back at the farm. His younger brother Mose would have to make do without him for a few hours. He could have said no to Elmer Miller's request that he pick up the new schoolteacher at the bus station, but he did his duty. Marcus Yoder always did his duty.

Elmer had slapped him on the back at the last Sunday church service. "Any chance you could pick up our pretty new schoolteacher at the West Union bus station on Tuesday?"

Marcus had laughed along with Elmer. Neither of them knew if the new schoolteacher was pretty or not. But there was a hesitation under Marcus's friendly chuckle. He had so much to do—and now he was supposed to take time out of the day to travel to the station and back?

He had been kept abreast of the search, since he lived in the farm across from the schoolhouse, and five of his siblings attended classes. Dat* had passed away five years ago, when Marcus was sixteen, barely out of school himself. Mose had been fourteen that year, and still in the eighth grade. Mose had helped on the farm in the mornings and evenings, because Mam had not wanted Mose to quit school, even as she had wanted to hold on to the farm. The community had wholeheartedly supported both decisions. Widows were always properly cared for in any Amish community, but the task was easier on everyone if some means of ready support could be found. That had translated into carrying on with Dat's farm, and continuing to milk the cows, a burden that had fallen heavily upon his young shoulders. Mam had noticed, and so had a few others, but life went on. He supposed it was easy to forget a young boy in the hustle and bustle of their busy community life.

Elmer's slap on the back last Sunday had been more than good-natured teasing. Elmer's eyes had twinkled. Elmer was

_____
* The Amish often refer to parents as "Dat" and "Mam."

telling him, "There is another duty you have, young man. It's time you find yourself a wife."

Marcus nodded respectfully, knowing that it would be disrespectful to tell the chairman of the school board that he was too busy to do this simple task for the community.

How was he supposed to find a wife when the duties of the farm lay so heavy on his back? There was hardly time for the weekly youth gatherings, and he never traveled into town in the early afternoon. Not without a special reason, like today. He did not live a carefree life. He knew the full weight of responsibility that most adults bore.

Marcus pulled his buggy to a stop and looked both ways before crossing another small bridge. The tinkling sound of the water soothed his soul. There were few moments these days when he had a chance to stop and listen to water flowing over rocks. He used to enjoy such things, and had often stepped barefoot into a stream on summer days. But that had been another life, light-years removed from his duties of supporting Mam, Mose, and four other siblings.

He supposed Elmer was right. He should think about a wife. When such thoughts crossed his mind late at night, he figured he wanted a serious girl, if he began dating. He wanted a woman who would stand beside him in the rough spots of life. There had been a few such girls in the community who he'd thought would meet that standard, but in each case by the time he came around to asking her for a date, another man had beaten him to the question. In his heart, he had often hoped one of them would wait for him, but none of the girls did. Maybe they didn't notice his attraction to them? He should move faster, and make his intentions known earlier, which was likely what Elmer had in mind with the trip today. This would be his chance to get a foot in the door first.

"Mary Wagler." Marcus spoke the new schoolteacher's name out of the buggy door. The only sound which came back was the steady beat of his horse's hooves on the pavement.

What was this Mary Wagler like? She must be dedicated to her duties, as a schoolteacher should be. Mary was young, he knew that much. Younger than he was. There had been nothing said in the exchange of letters between the school board and Mary Wagler about a boyfriend. Elmer wouldn't have sent him on this errand if there had been.

Marcus let his breath out slowly. Was the truth really that he was scared of starting a friendship with a young woman? That did not make the least bit of sense. He had plenty of courage for everyday living, and dating and marriage in the community were very much a part of everyday living. He must look at dating as a necessity, something that must be done. He must gather his courage, and venture across the waters. The Lord was working things out for him in His own way, so he had best take the gentle nudge Elmer had given him.

"Mary Wagler," he said again. Could Mary Wagler be his future wife? Could he ask her for a date? At least he knew what he wanted in a wife—stability, a woman who could get by on a tight budget and be happy with her state in life. Most of the girls in the community were like that. That's what being Amish was about, so there was no reason to think that Mary Wagler would be any different.

"Mary Wagler," Marcus said again, and settled into his buggy seat. Now he was so nervous he could barely see the road in front of him.

Twenty minutes later the bus lurched over the curb and lumbered to a stop. Mary leaped to her feet, her bonnet askew, as the bus drive announced, "West Union."

Finally! She had arrived. Mary bent over to peer out of the dusty windows. There was a buggy parked on the far side of the gas station, but no Amish women or men were in sight. Maybe they waited inside for her? She grasped the seat to steady herself and made her way up the aisle.

"You have luggage," the bus driver stated more than asked.

"Yah!" Mary offered him her sweetest smile.

He didn't return the favor. "I'll have your luggage out in a moment."

What made the man so rude? She had paid to transport the extra suitcase, so there was no reason for short tempers, or snootiness. She didn't want to arrive destitute in a new community, or fail to make a proper impression because she wore the same dress at the schoolhouse every day.

Mary followed the driver down the steps and paused on the last one. Should she? Yah, she would. With a leap Mary completed her journey to the ground, and ended upright with arms waving. That was a perfect, proper entry into her new life. If the school board wives saw her execute the maneuver through the glass of the gas station's waiting room, they would understand perfectly, and certainly appreciate their adventurous and creative new schoolteacher.

"Thank you, dear Lord, for bringing me here," Mary proclaimed out loud. She didn't care who heard.

Marcus stood beside the bus driver, helping to unload the suitcases from the hatch. He stared at the Amish girl who catapulted herself out of the bus door and pronounced a prayer of thanks with her head lifted towards the heavens. The words hung for a moment in the air of the parking lot. Beautiful words they were, but they had been spoken in public by a woman.

The bus driver shrugged, as if nothing surprised him, and dug deeper into the luggage compartment. There were already two suitcases on the ground. Mary Wagler's piece must be buried deep.

The bus driver grunted and pulled another suitcase out. "There," he said. "That's it."

Marcus bent low to read the names. They all said, "Mary Wagler," plain enough, written in beautiful cursive, on pink name tags. The last suitcase pulled from the hatch was a shimmering shade of blue.

He turned and stared at the approaching Amish girl. She was pretty beyond belief, slender as a willow branch and smiling as if the sun had just risen on a perfect day.

"Mary Wagler," she said, extending her hand. "Who are you?" She laughed. "I mean, you are Amish, obviously, but why are you here?"

"You are the new schoolteacher," he said, as if that explained everything.

The bus driver cleared his throat. "If that's it, Ms. Wagler, I'll be going."

She took in her suitcases with a quick glance. "That's it. Thank you."

The bus driver scurried off without a backward glance.

"So where's my ride?" Mary was looking around the parking lot. "Are the school board women waiting inside?"

Marcus's mouth worked soundlessly for a few moments. "I am your ride."

Her pretty face wrinkled in disapproval. "Now don't we say!"

He squared his shoulders. Elmer had sent him, and he had done nothing wrong.

"Don't forget your glowing suitcase," he ordered, grasping the other two. Every bit of his nervousness had fled far away. If she could disapprove of him, he could return the favor. Why did she have so much stuff? Three suitcases, including that ridiculous bright turquoise one. So she was the kind of woman who wanted to draw attention to herself with fancy things, who loved excessive belongings. His earlier musings of a woman who might be a suitable match for him suddenly seemed incredibly foolish as irritation clouded his thoughts. Why had he allowed himself to hope? His disappointment manifested as annoyance. "Do you always travel with enough luggage for a family?"

CHAPTER 2

MARY WAGLER DRAGGED HER TURQUOISE BLUE SUITCASE ON ITS wheels across the rough pavement of the gas station parking lot. The broad back of the Amish man walking in front of her was squared and muscled. Both of her heavy suitcases were hoisted in the air as if they weighed mere ounces. The man obviously disdained to use the much easier method of wheeling them across the pavement. Perhaps he didn't know that suitcases had wheels? The dunce! Why had he had to insult her about her luggage when she had offered him such a pleasant greeting?

The man was arrogant and full of himself. Why had he come to meet her at the bus stop, alone? Surely there were other women in the town who could have come, or at least accompanied him. But wait a minute. She knew why. He had volunteered in the hopes of snagging an early foothold on her affections. Impress her with his gentlemanly willingness to transport a hapless schoolteacher to her new lodgings! What a thick head the man had, to think that such a lowbrow trick would work on her, even if he had managed to show his charming side—if he had one, which she'd seen no evidence of thus far. He hadn't even bothered to introduce himself.

Perhaps he thought his unjustified disapproval of her traveling methods would cow her into submission? He hadn't hesitated a second before making that caustic remark about traveling with enough luggage for a whole family.

She was surprised he knew the word "luggage." Most Amish men spoke of suitcases, or bags. At least he wasn't totally uneducated.

The man broke his stride to lower her luggage to the ground and unlatch the back door of his buggy. With a heave, he hurled the suitcases inside. She cringed. Those were her best dresses, but she was not about to lower herself to an objection. She would just have to hang them as soon as she arrived to get the wrinkles out.

He turned to look at the suitcase she had wheeled across the parking lot. Clearly there was not enough room in the back of the buggy.

"You'll have to balance the thing at your feet," he said, not meeting her gaze. "There isn't room."

She bit back a sharp retort. *Why didn't you bring a bigger buggy?*

"By the way, my name is Marcus," he said, looking quite impatient.

"Why are you meeting me instead of the school board wives?"

"Elmer Miller asked me to come. I live next door to the schoolhouse, as do Leon and Lavina Hochstetler, where you will board."

"I know about Leon and Lavina Hochstetler," she said.

"I suppose you do. Shall we go?" He motioned with his square, shaven chin towards the buggy door. "Half of your pretty suitcase will hang over the side."

"And that's a problem?"

"It can't be helped," he said, as if she hadn't spoken. "The weather is nice, so the door doesn't have to close."

"I know that," she snapped.

"We'll get there fine," he said. "Shall I help you?"

She didn't answer, carefully lifting the suitcase into the buggy with both hands and clambering up after it.

He had an amused expression on his face after he untied his horse and climbed into the buggy. She was sure his mirth wasn't expended on the ridiculous sight they made—driving out of the gas station parking lot with her suitcase dangled half out the door. She almost wished she hadn't been so daring and purchased the turquoise blue one for the trip. The decision had seemed appropriate at the time, befitting her new start in life and venture into un-sailed waters. Mam's old brown one, stored in the attic, would have been the wiser choice. Well, there wasn't much to be done about it now. She was allowed a few innocent mistakes, wasn't she? This was all so new—she couldn't be expected to get everything exactly right.

"Whoa there," Marcus called out to Rowdy as a light in downtown West Union turned red.

He didn't dare glance at Mary seated on the buggy seat beside him. His courage was seeping away. The woman's beauty and presence were overwhelming. He shouldn't have been so disapproving of her luggage back at the gas station, but his reaction had been instinctual. If Mary only knew how much he hadn't wanted to make the drive into West Union with the press of the farm's evening chores on his schedule, she might be more understanding. Of course, he couldn't tell her the whole truth. Yah, he had made the trip to accommodate Elmer, but there had been a tiny hope in his heart that perhaps Elmer's teasing had a base in reality. That perhaps his time had arrived to impress a decent, solid, hardworking Amish woman.

He was more disappointed than he wanted to admit. Mary was not even an option to date, let alone marry. She was far too beautiful for him, plus she was haughty and vain. Not that that gave him a right to rudeness, regardless of how she had acted.

Marcus took a deep breath and jiggled the reins. The light had turned green. An apology was in order, but he couldn't bring himself to say the words.

"Is the suitcase staying inside?" he inquired instead as Rowdy trotted down the street.

"It is," she said, not looking at him.

"How was your journey?"

"Okay." Her voice was terse.

"I don't like bus travel much."

"Have you traveled often?"

He kept his eyes on the road. "Our family visited Holmes County a few years ago."

"I see," she said. "Was the experience bad?"

"The bus was stopping and starting all the time. I grew a little impatient, I guess."

"I prayed for patience on the trip down," she said, "and the Lord granted my cry."

He prickled at the preachy tone in her voice. "I had my reasons for not liking the trip," he said.

"Prayer is a great spiritual exercise," she intoned, obviously thinking he needed the lecture. "It's difficult at times, even for me, but in the end the fruits borne are from the Lord."

He gritted his teeth.

"I prayed long and hard about my desire to teach in another community," she continued, "and the Lord answered beautifully. I knew I was coming to Adams County the moment I saw that ad in *The Budget*."

"I didn't know there was an ad."

"I thought you would know, given that the school board trusted you with meeting their new schoolteacher at the bus stop."

He pressed his lips together. Explaining was useless. If Mary knew that he had imagined a date with her, he would never live down the embarrassment.

"I don't know everything," he said instead.

"Are you going to be nice to me now?"

He grimaced. "I shouldn't have said what I did about your luggage, but why do you have *three* pieces of luggage?"

Her nose went into the air. "You are not going to be nice to me."

"It's just a question. I was wondering."

"I needed three," she retorted. "You don't think I did?"

He shrugged. "Like I said, I don't know everything."

Mary's gaze was focused on the protruding suitcase.

"You can pull it in further," he offered, moving his feet to the side.

She jerked the handle, and the suitcase slammed against his shoes.

"Sorry," she said, looking like she really was. She tried to move the suitcase to the left again.

"I'm okay," he said.

"This is better," she muttered, gazing out of the buggy door.

He clutched the reins as they came to a stop sign. He had never sat this close to a beautiful girl before.

Out of the corner of her eye, Mary watched Marcus's hands grip the reins. He was quite handsome, and on the surface appeared likable. Too bad that appearances didn't give the true picture. Clearly Marcus was as unimpressed with her as she was with him.

"How far do we have to go yet?" she asked.

"A few miles."

"And you live next door to where I will board?"

"I do. I have five siblings who attend classes."

"That's nice." She tried to smile. "I'm sure they enjoy school."

"They always have," he said.

She looked away. He had his nerve, but she already knew that.

"I'm sure you'll do okay," he continued.

"I'm sure I will," she shot back.

He smiled, a tolerating sort of smile, as if her presence must be borne with great patience.

Mary focused her gaze out of the buggy door. They were crossing a small stream, with the water tinkling as they passed. There was no sense quarreling with the man. In the grand scheme of things, his opinion did not matter. What the parents of her students and the school board thought was what she would concern herself with. They would not be like Marcus. Not even close. She was sure of that.

"School was a good time for me," he said, as if the subject should be changed.

"Everyone enjoys their school years, if they have a decent teacher." She made sure there was plenty of emphasis on the word "teacher."

"I had that," he said. "Nancy Miller was my teacher for most of the grades. She got married the year after I left school."

"Does Nancy still live around here?"

"She's Eli Glick's wife," he said. "Life moves on."

"It does," she agreed. "But not all schoolteachers have to marry."

"I suppose not." He shook the reins.

"Do you disagree?"

"I don't know. Most do marry."

"And why is that?"

"I don't know, just saying."

"They don't have to," she said.

He shrugged and didn't answer.

"The will of God does not always include getting married."

"Perhaps," he allowed. "There are occasions when that is true, but not often for our people."

"So you think a woman should marry just because it's time to marry?"

"You are asking me?"

"You seem to have plenty of opinions to offer on other things . . . like luggage."

"I shouldn't have spoken so plainly."

"But you still thought your opinions?"

"Does that make me a criminal, thinking a woman shouldn't run around the country with an overabundance of shimmering luggage?"

Mary bristled, feeling her cheeks flush. "Do you think that's why I'm not married?"

He didn't answer, obviously pretending to concentrate on his driving.

"You can tell me," she finally said, more softly now. Did he detect a note of sadness in her voice?

"My guess is that you've had plenty of offers to date."

She raised her eyebrows at him.

"I would be right," he said. "Yah!"

"That was not what I asked."

"But I am right."

"And why do you think that is?"

He pressed his lips together. "We are about there."

"I would like to know," she insisted.

"What does my opinion matter, if I even have one?"

"I'm sure you do. You think I should be dating?"

He pulled back on the reins. "I'm surprised that you're not."

"Do you mean that in a nice way, or . . ."

"Do you always ask this many questions?"

"I'm a teacher."

He gave her suitcase a skeptical look.

"Are you going to judge me forever by my suitcases?"

"It shimmers," he said. "Suitcases shouldn't shimmer."

She forced a smile and stayed silent this time. The man was hopeless.

"Whoa there," Marcus called out to Rowdy as he made the turn deftly into the Hochstetlers' driveway. He pulled to a stop by the barn, glad the drive and the questions were over. He could hardly breathe properly with her on the buggy seat beside him.

"We're here," he said, trying to sound friendly.

Mary appeared to have forgotten their conversation as she leaned out of the buggy to inspect the place. "What a beautiful setting Leon and Lavina have, and that must be the schoolhouse? Right?"

"Right," he said, climbing down.

"And that must be your home across the fields?" She lightly leaped to the ground after him.

"It is," he said.

She stood, staring rapturously at the schoolhouse while he tied Rowdy to the hitching post.

CHAPTER 3

Mary pasted on her brightest smile on the walk from the barn to the white two-story house. Behind her, she could hear the steady tread of Marcus Yoder, his arms laden with her two heaviest suitcases. If not for the fuss, she would have insisted that he leave them by the barn and carried them up the sidewalks herself later.

But this would be her new home for the next nine months. Banishing her next-door neighbor and leaving suitcases sitting in the barnyard while his buggy rattled out the driveway was not the way she wished to begin her stay in the community. Better to expect that Lavina Hochstetler was a gracious and understanding host, even to a girl who walked in with three suitcases, including a turquoise blue one. Marcus's critical attitude must be the exception in this place. If not, her future was filled with the dark clouds of a disapproving thunderstorm. She couldn't believe the Lord had led her into such nasty weather.

She must have faith. She had prayed, and the Lord would not let her down. Mary snuck a quick glance over her shoulder, but Marcus didn't return her smile. Maybe he knew that hers was a pasted-one one?

The front door opened in front of her, and a round-faced woman stepped out, clad in a dark blue dress. Lavina Hochstetler squinted for a moment before the smile came, followed by the hurried steps forward.

"Our new schoolteacher! Yah!" Lavina exclaimed. "Why didn't I hear anyone drive in the lane?"

"I sneak in like a mouse into the barn," Marcus quipped.

Lavina waved her hand dismissively at him and opened her arms wide for Mary. "I hope Marcus gave you a proper Adams County welcome."

"He got me here quite safely," Mary managed.

Lavina held her at arm's length. "Let me look at you. My, you are a lovely thing, and so young. Our new schoolteacher."

"I am so glad to meet you," Mary demurred, her smile still in place.

"And I'm glad to meet you. I hope our home is to your satisfaction."

"I'm sure it is. You have a lovely place."

"Thanks." Lavina smiled. "We try to keep the farm up. Leon is getting on in years, but Marcus is across the road and takes a great load off of our minds. If there should be an emergency, he is always there."

"I'm sure he is," Mary said, not looking at him. Her private feelings about Marcus Yoder had best stay buried.

"But you don't have to take care of everything." Lavina was looking accusingly at Marcus. "Why did you pick Mary up at the bus station? If you had let me know I would have gone."

"Elmer asked me to," Marcus said, setting down the suitcases. "I should be going."

"It was very sweet of Marcus to make the trip, and take the time out of his busy schedule," Mary said. She should at least be courteous to the man.

Lavina cast quick glances between the two of them, obviously drawing the wrong conclusions. To make matters worse, Marcus had turned bright red and beat a hasty retreat.

Both of them watched Marcus leap into his buggy and whirl out of the lane.

"He is such a nice man," Lavina said. "I'm sure you have discovered that on the drive in from town."

"He did pick me up at the bus station." Mary avoided the question.

Lavina still appeared quite pleased. "I'm glad you got to meet Marcus right off and become acquainted. When he agreed to pick you up, Marcus made the right choice in more ways than one."

"I think he was just doing his duty," Mary said quickly. "The chairman of the school board, after all, did ask him to meet me at the bus station."

Lavina's look of satisfaction didn't fade. "Either way, Marcus got to meet you the day you arrived. I'm glad for that." Lavina reached for one of the suitcases and Mary picked up the other two. "Come on in the house, and we'll get you settled. Supper is at six. I hope that's soon enough. You must be starved after your travels."

"I am hungry," Mary admitted, "but six is fine."

Lavina opened the door into a large living room, with a kitchen going off to the right and a sewing room situated on the left. Deeper in there was a sitting room, and a bedroom door. The steps to the second level went up without a stairwell, and the basement stairs were around the corner from the kitchen.

"Your room is upstairs." Lavina was all smiles. "And this is our home."

"It is lovely. Absolutely perfect!" Mary declared.

Marcus unhitched Rowdy in the barnyard across the road, his gaze drifting frequently towards the Hochstetlers' place. The trip home from West Union with the new schoolteacher seated beside him seemed like a dream—a disconcerting dream. Yet he was sure it had happened. He had dropped Mary off at the Hochstetlers' place moments ago.

"What was she like?" his younger brother Mose came out of the barn to ask.

Marcus grabbed Rowdy's bridle with both hands and led the horse forward.

Mose laughed. "I guess that answers my question."

"I was thinking," Marcus retorted.

"Some thinking," Mose chuckled. "The new schoolteacher must be awfully pretty. Did you make any headways gaining her affections?"

"I went to pick up Mary Wagler because Elmer asked me to go," he snapped.

Mose grinned from ear to ear. "So she is prettier than any of the girls around here?"

"I drove Mary home from the bus station," Marcus retorted. "That's all you need to know."

Mose reached for the bridle. "Let me take Rowdy into the barn for you. After such a dramatic experience you must need time to rest and recover in the house."

Marcus handed over the horse and didn't protest. He was to blame for the teasing Mose gave him, and for the further ribbing he would receive at the Sunday services. Mary was beautiful, but she was not for him. He could mention that fact in response to the teasing, but no one would believe him. They would think he had used the ride home from the bus station to work his charms on the community's new schoolteacher.

What charms? He didn't have any, and didn't need any. Charms weren't necessary with the kind of wife he wanted. People would have to draw the conclusions they wished. He should have thought of that sooner and resisted the temptation Elmer had offered him. That's what Mary was, a temptation. He would not succumb. Mary was here to teach school, and that was where his interest in her began and ended. He would see her frequently, since he was the janitor at the schoolhouse and five of his siblings attended classes, but he would harbor no further fancy ideas about her being his future wife. The Lord had better ways in which to work His will.

Visions of Mary's shimmering suitcase floated in front of his eyes, and Marcus pushed them away. There was no way he wanted a wife who traveled with such outlandish luggage.

Marcus determinedly lifted his chin before he entered the front door of the Yoders' house and headed towards his bedroom to change. Before he reached the stairs, his mother stopped him with her appearance in the kitchen doorway.

"How did it go?" she asked with wistfulness in her voice.

Marcus winced. He had not mentioned a word to Mam about anything romantic when he left the house to pick Mary up at the bus station. "Mam," he chided.

"Is she decent?"

"All schoolteachers are decent," he said. Mary would likely be very competent and well-mannered in the classroom. He would grant her that much.

"It is not right, the way you sacrifice your life for this family," Mam said. "It is time that you began one on your own."

"I do what is right," he said. "I'm not complaining."

"Was she at all . . ." Mam hesitated. "Suitable? Did you feel an interest in the girl? A little?"

Marcus forced a laugh. "What do you expect? An angel to fly in from heaven and sweep me off my feet?"

"I am serious, Marcus," she said.

"Did Elmer speak with you?" he asked.

Mam nodded. "What he said was true. My eyes have been blinded. I've been thinking too much about myself since Dat passed. Letting you carry a load which doesn't belong on your shoulders."

"I'm okay. I really am."

"I have accepted a date this weekend with John Beachy," she said.

Marcus stared. "John Beachy, the widower."

"It is time. I have to move on. John asked me a few months ago, but I turned him down. I shouldn't have. The man waited for me, even when I had given him no hope."

"Mam!" he exclaimed. "This is wrong. You don't really want to start a friendship with him or you would have accepted his offer earlier."

"That is not true. I told Elmer to pass on the word that I was willing to date him, if John was still interested."

"Of course he's interested!" Marcus seized her arm. "Mam. Don't do this because of me. I'm okay. I'm happy."

"You are not the only one who does what is right." She smiled gently. "I know what love is, thanks to your dat. I will not marry a man I cannot love."

He looked away.

"So Mary was decent?"

"Mam, please."

"It is time that you found a wife."

"Mam," he said again.

"Was she interested in you?"

He reached for the stair doorknob and propelled himself upward. When he glanced over his shoulder, Mam still stood at the bottom. She peered hopefully up after him. Mam's pleadings would not change his opinion of Mary Wagler. He entered his room and pulled the door shut behind him.

Mary lingered in the upstairs bedroom of the Hochstetler home after Lavina had left.

"Take your time settling in," Lavina had told her. "I have supper under control, so you don't have to help."

"I'll be down soon," Mary had replied.

She liked Lavina, and had liked her from the moment they met. After Marcus's disapproval, the Lord would not lay a heavier burden on her shoulders than she could bear. Lavina would make living in the community a joy and delight.

Mary pushed back the drapes on the window to look out in the direction of the schoolhouse. The structure was rectangular with white shiplapped siding. A bell tower was perched on top. She could already hear the clanging of the bell after each recess, and the eager voices of her students vying for the privilege of pulling the cord.

"Can I? Please, teacher," they would beg.

"You will take turns," she would tell them. Disappointment would cross their faces, but so much greater would be their happiness when their opportunity arrived.

Mary let the drapes slip from her fingers and heaved the turquoise suitcase onto the bed. She opened the zipper and took out the first of her dresses. The nerve of Marcus. She had stuck up for him in front of Lavina, but Marcus wouldn't have had to follow Elmer's suggestion. She knew what had happened. Marcus had arrived at the bus station with hope in his heart, thinking this might be a chance to meet his future wife. She had not been fooled. Obviously Marcus had decided rather quickly that she did not fit his vision of a wife. At least the man could make up his mind. But she was not going to allow Marcus's opinion to mar her future in the community. He was nothing to her, a man who lived across the road. That was all.

Mary lifted her face to the ceiling and let the happiness of this place wash over her. "Thank you, Lord, for bringing me here," she whispered.

Mary opened the closet door to hang the dresses and stuffed the empty blue suitcase into the farthest corner. When she walked over to the window again, another buggy had pulled in the driveway. She watched the man climb out and approach the house. A moment later Lavina called up the stairs, "Someone is here to see you!"

Mary hurried out of the bedroom.

"Elmer Miller," Lavina mouthed at the bottom of the stairs. "He's waiting outside on the porch."

There was a twinkle in Elmer's eyes when she opened the door. "Elmer Miller." He extended his hand. "Welcome to the community."

"Thanks." She smiled.

"I see Marcus got you here safely."

"Yep, and thanks for setting up the ride."

"Everything going well with the Hochstetlers?"

"Perfectly."

"Our former schoolteacher, Susie Martin, will meet you at eight tomorrow morning at the schoolhouse to go over the lessons and curriculum we use. If that works for you?"

"Works for me."

"Sounds like everything is in hand then," he said. "We are honored to have you, and welcome again."

"Thanks for hiring me."

He grinned. "You haven't met everyone yet."

Mary laughed. "I'm sure they are more than pleasant, and the children will be darlings to work with."

"Spoken like a true schoolteacher," he said, appearing pleased. "You have a *goot** night, then."

"And you, too," she said, and he left, driving his buggy out of the lane.

Moments later, Marcus exited the Yoders' house in his chore clothing. He paused at the sight of Elmer's buggy approaching the driveway. Marcus waited until Elmer pulled to a stop at the hitching post before he walked up to the buggy.

"How are you doing?" Elmer leaned out of the door with a big grin on his face.

---

*   *goot* is the Pennsylvania Dutch word for "good."

"Okay." Marcus's shoe toe dug into the gravel of the drive-way. The teasing had only just begun.

"Mary will be at the schoolhouse to meet Susie at eight," Elmer said. "You should get the fire going in the morning, as cool as the nights have been."

"I'll do that."

Elmer lingered. "I didn't tell her that you are the janitor. I figured you got that all straight on your ride home."

Marcus stared. "I don't think we talked about who was janitor."

"So how did the ride home go?" Elmer was obviously per-plexed. "She seems like an awesome girl, quite suitable . . ."

"Mary should make a perfect schoolteacher," he said. "I'm sure the school board didn't make a mistake."

Elmer still appeared confused. "Mary looks like she is much more than that. I hope you make the most of your opportunity which the Lord has given you."

Marcus tried to smile. There was no way he was going to spread rumors in the community about Mary's shimmering suit-case or flighty ways. The woman wasn't suitable marriage mate-rial for him, but that didn't mean that another man wouldn't snatch her up in a moment. The woman was beautiful—gor-geous, in fact. Mary should have no lack of suitors, that much was clear.

"You have a good evening then." Elmer jiggled the reins. "And don't be leaving Mary unattended for long. She deserves a *goot* man like you."

The objection choked in Marcus's throat, but Elmer didn't seem to notice. He turned his buggy around in the driveway, and with a wave of his hand was gone. Marcus gathered himself together and entered the barn to let the heavy door slam behind him. Mose had the cows in their stanchions, with the feed shov-eled into the wheelbarrow, ready for distribution.

"I'll take things from here," he told his brother.

Mose's eyes twinkled. "She was pretty, wasn't she?"

"You'll find out soon enough," he retorted, and grabbed the shovel from Mose's hand.

"Wow," Mose said. "I can't wait to meet this Mary."

Marcus busied himself with his chores and ignored his brother. There had been enough thinking and talking about Mary Wagler for one day.

CHAPTER 4

THAT FOLLOWING MORNING MARY WAGLER AWOKE WITH A START. She sat bolt upright in the strange bed, with the covers flying. She stared at the alarm clock. Five thirty! She had awakened on her own. Mary stilled the rapid beat of her heart as excitement rushed through her. Awakening early in this new place was an excellent sign and a promise of a great day ahead. She had rested well, after the hearty supper served last night by Lavina. The meal had been eaten to the tune of happy conversation and laughter as she had become better acquainted with the elderly couple. Leon, with his lengthy salt-and-pepper beard, had proven as charming and good-natured as his wife. The Lord had truly blessed her with a place to call home away from home.

Mary punched the button on the alarm clock to turn it off before she pushed back the drapes. The dawn was rising on the horizon, a deep blush of red light that bubbled up from the other side of the world. The white schoolhouse lay in the middle, beckoning and calling her. The sight overwhelmed her.

"The world could not be more beautiful this morning," she whispered. "Thank you, dear Lord."

Mary lingered for a long time at the window before she lit the kerosene lamp and dressed for the day. On schedule was a workday with Susie at the schoolhouse, so she wouldn't wear her best dress, but come Monday morning she would have a line of proper Sunday dresses to wear which were suitable attire for a schoolteacher. No one would assume she came from an impoverished family who couldn't afford decent clothing, or worse, that she had wasted her money since she became of age at twenty-one.

Mary blew out the lamp and left the bedroom to make her way down the dark stairs, her fingers pressed against the wall. There was enough light from the open stairwell to find her way. The smell of a delicious breakfast drifted upward, wafting around her face. She stepped into the light of the lantern, making sure her steps creaked on the hardwood floor. She didn't want to startle Lavina.

Lavina looked up from her work at the stove with a bright smile. "*Goot* morning. Hope you slept well?"

"Your home is *wunderbah**," Mary assured her. "I am so grateful that you and Leon have given me a place to stay."

"And we are thankful that you came down to teach the children of our beloved community." Lavina gave a little laugh. "We have lived here our whole lives. Most of them are related to us one way or the other. That's why new schoolteachers are greeted with such eagerness."

Mary smiled. "Your kindness is appreciated just the same. How can I help with breakfast?"

"I'm thinking you made quite the impression on Marcus yesterday." Lavina ignored Mary's question. *Already?* she thought. *Do we have to talk about Marcus first thing in the morning?*

Mary tried to keep her smile in place. "He is handsome enough."

"I know, and still single. Isn't that something? The Lord moves in mysterious ways." Lavina beamed.

"I . . . I don't think things went quite like Marcus planned," she managed. It was time to put a stop to these expectations before they got out of hand.

---

* Pennsylvania Dutch word for "wonderful."

"Really?"

"He wasn't very impressed, I don't think."

Lavina looked quite unconvinced. "You expect me to believe that?"

"I'm not being modest. Marcus didn't like much about me."

"I'm sorry to hear that. I need to speak with the man."

"Please don't," Mary gasped. "I didn't mean to criticize Marcus."

Lavina appeared ready to say more when the outside door below the kitchen burst open, and Leon entered.

"*Goot* morning," he hollered up the stairwell. "What is this *wunderbah* smell that floats down to hang around my nose?"

"Just breakfast cooking, dear."

"Something special, it seems, for someone special."

"That would be you," Lavina hollered back.

"Be right up," Leon said, and went down the basement stairs.

"Can I help with something?" Mary offered again.

"Set the table, perhaps," Lavina suggested. "You know where we sit from last night."

Mary moved quickly and the plates and silverware were in place by the time Lavina finished with the eggs and bacon. There was a pot of oatmeal kept warm on a corner of the stove. Leon appeared moments later, his face still aglow from his morning chores. "The Lord has given us a beautiful day," he proclaimed, seating himself.

"That He has," Lavina agreed.

"Amen." Mary echoed. "I was watching the sunrise from my window. I can't say how thankful I am for how the Lord has led me down here, and how lovely this house is. I slept like I was at home."

"That's what we want to hear." Leon grinned from ear to ear. "Shall we pray and bless the food?"

Lavina transferred the plate of eggs and took a chair. "I'm ready."

They bowed their heads in silent prayer.

"I haven't seen Marcus head up to the schoolhouse this morning," Leon observed. "It's chilly enough for a fire, I'm thinking."

Mary tried to hide her surprise. Why was Marcus responsible for fires in the schoolhouse?

"Marcus takes his duties seriously," Lavina said. "He'll be up before eight, when Mary has to meet Susie."

"I'm sure he will be," Leon said, his eyes twinkling. "Didn't Marcus bring you home last night?"

"Leon," Lavina chided. "I've already been over that with Mary this morning. Marcus needs a talking-to, I think."

Leon didn't appear to get the hint. "I think this is in many ways a day of new beginnings, for all of us, but especially for Marcus. The man has waited a long time for his gift from heaven."

A rush of red spread across Mary's face. She helped herself to the bacon and eggs, then quickly changed the subject. "This is truly a great breakfast. Thank you, so very much."

Mary saw Lavina pinch Leon on the arm, leading to a puzzled look that never quite left his face, even as the talk turned to chores and plans for the day. Lavina would have to explain later. This wasn't the time to venture into the troubled waters that surrounded Marcus Yoder.

Marcus made his way across the hayfield with the sun bright in his eyes. He tipped his hat to shield his face and turned sideways to open the wooden gate into the schoolyard.

He should have come down an hour ago to light the fire, but he had to admit to himself that he wanted to see Mary again. Elmer's words bothered him more than he wished to acknowledge. "Don't be leaving Mary unattended." Surely he wasn't missing the Lord's will? Elmer was his elder, and was usually right, but Elmer didn't know what he knew. Mary was simply not an option. She was much too beautiful to take an interest in him, and her attitude and incessant questions were intolerable. So why did he wish to see her again this morning? Simply to confirm that his first impression had not been off the mark, he told himself. And perhaps to make amends for his initial rudeness, which he couldn't deny. He hadn't meant to make her uncomfortable, but he had, and that wasn't right, regardless of how odd and *grosfeelich** she was. Anyway, he had to visit the schoolhouse to fulfill his duties, and a tense relationship between the two of them would benefit no one, so he may as well try to make her feel welcome.

He pulled the schoolhouse key from his pocket and unlocked the front door. When he stepped inside, the chill of the large room swept over him. He hurried to the stove and set a match to the kindling he had prepared last week. The flames leaped upward quickly and he added larger pieces of wood before he closed the stove door. The smoke puffed from the pipe and Marcus worked the damper a few times to find the best rate of draw. Warmth crept outward from the stove and he opened his coat.

While Marcus waited, he looked around the schoolroom. His years spent here as a student seemed light-years away this morning, almost as if they had never happened. He had learned the lessons that could be learned, but the real lessons that life taught had been etched in sorrow and pain on his heart, after Dat's passing. Those were not things presented in a schoolhouse, things which were hardly teachable at a student's desk. How could a book show a young child what life was like without his father, or measure the weight of the world that would settle on his shoulders?

Marcus ran his fingers over the back of the closest well-built desk. The faint outlines of initials made their presence

---

* Pennsylvania Dutch word meaning arrogant, prideful.

felt underneath his fingers. He hadn't carved his name into the wood when he went to school. Such a prank was not allowed by the rules. A few of the boys chose to act out on their baser instincts anyway, taking the chance they wouldn't get caught by the teacher.

Would Mary be sharp enough to catch such childhood pranks? Likely not. She was a teacher who would become so deeply enraptured in her lessons that she lost track of childhood natures on rampage around her. Some rash eighth-grader might even light the match which could burn down the place. Marcus grimaced. That was a bit extreme, but Mary was flighty. There was no question there.

The schoolhouse door opened behind him, and Marcus turned around.

Mary was glaring up at him. "Why are you still here?"

"I'm sorry, I forgot to tell you yesterday that I'm the janitor," he said. Her tone was already caustic, but he pushed away the instinct to reply with a defensive retort.

"You drove me home yesterday in your buggy. There was plenty of time."

"You are right," he admitted. "I should have told you."

"That's what comes from being critical of luggage."

"I was hoping we could leave that behind us, and begin anew," he said.

"And how is that?"

"As friends," he said quickly. "I am the janitor and I do have to come up to the schoolhouse."

"So you are changing your opinion about my luggage?"

"I'm keeping it to myself," he said. "You have a right to arrive with whatever color suitcase you desire."

"So do you have more criticism for me this morning? Perhaps doubts about my school teaching skills?"

Now he was starting to struggle. Here he was, humbling himself and making an honest attempt to be civil, and all she could do was poke and probe him with accusatory questions? He forced a slow breath to calm himself, which she interpreted as disapproval.

"I see." She tilted her head at him.

"I do have strong opinions," he admitted, as calmly as possible, "but I did mean what I said about the fresh start between us."

"So you envision a future in which you hold your dark opinions of me privately."

"Must you misconstrue everything I say? I am trying."

Mary softened a little and smiled grimly. "I guess you are the janitor, and we will need to get along. I will be nice, which is easy for me, and you will think nice thoughts about me, which is difficult for you. Do you think we can manage that?" It came out sounding far more condescending than she'd intended, but she couldn't take it back now.

"Look," he said, "I was tasked with bringing you home from the bus station, and I should have been focusing on that—on your comfort—rather than concerning myself with your belongings."

"So we are back to the suitcases."

Marcus sighed in frustration, realizing anything he said would be twisted. It was better not to respond at all. Didn't the Bible say, "He that refraineth his lips is wise"?

"You are right," Mary conceded, to his surprise. "Maybe we should leave yesterday alone."

He nodded.

"Well then," she said. "That's that."

"Susie just came." He glanced out of the schoolhouse window. "You can bank the fire when you're done."

Her irritation showed. "I'm not a dunce."

"I didn't mean to imply that you were."

"Just go." She dismissed him with a wave of her hand.

Just outside the door he met Susie as she was coming in. "*Goot* morning," Marcus greeted her hurriedly.

"Got the fire going as usual," Susie said, smiling broadly.

"Yep."

Susie lowered her voice. "What is the new teacher like?"

"She'll make a *goot* one, just like you did," he said, pulling his hat low over his eyes.

Susie tugged on his arm. "That's not what I meant."

Marcus yanked his arm loose and left Susie holding the door as he rushed across the field.

CHAPTER 5

Mary awoke again on Sunday morning without the alarm. Outside the window drapes the first signs of a pale dawn shimmered. There were soft puttering noises coming from downstairs. Lavina was up and busy with the breakfast preparations. Mary slipped out of bed and pushed back the drapes to gaze out at the ballooning sunrise. The day would be gorgeous, from the looks of things. This was her first Sunday in the community. How appropriate and blessed of the Lord to give her a clear day. Not that rain was a sign of the Lord's disapproval, but sunshine was better for her formal presentation to the parents of her students.

"You will love your time here in the community," Susie had assured her on Friday. "The people are *wunderbah*, and the parents are so understanding. Even when things don't go right."

"I'm sure the students are little angels," she had replied.

"They have been raised well," Susie had concurred.

Susie had been so helpful, and would remain on call if she needed further help. When they had finished going over the lessons, Susie had said with a twinkle in her eye, "That's a nice janitor we have. He's quite handsome."

Mary was sure a rush of color had betrayed her irritation. Marcus was well esteemed in the community, and she didn't want to criticize him. But was the whole town determined to set the two of them up together? Susie, of course, took her blush completely the wrong way.

"And he's so available," Susie gushed. "I got the best man in the community, but there's still *goot* ones available in our little pond."

"I came to teach school," she replied, perhaps more forcefully than she intended, but Susie's gleeful smile hadn't faded.

"See you on Sunday!" Susie had hollered before leaving, waving vigorously while driving out of the schoolyard.

The people she had met so far were certainly friendly, and seemed to like her. That was a great start, but Marcus lurked in the back of her mind like an impending storm cloud. Maybe he would stay true to his word, and their relationship could return to a respectful one, but she doubted it. The man had way too many opinions to keep them to himself. Such things could not be helped. She would have to make peace with his disapproval. At least Marcus was handsome. Better a handsome critic than a homely one.

Mary made a wry face at the window while she dressed, and hurried downstairs afterward. She peeked in the kitchen doorway. "*Goot* morning."

"Why are you up?" Lavina scolded.

"I'm helping with breakfast."

"That is totally unnecessary. I told you that."

Mary marched on in. "Are we going to argue on a Sunday morning?"

Lavina laughed. "The eggs are in the refrigerator. You already know how Leon likes them."

She did, and Lavina had trusted her to notice such things. Leon liked his eggs flipped in the pan at the first possible moment and taken out with the yolks still running. With someone as mild mannered and understanding as Leon, she might look forward to serving her own husband someday. The fun would be squashed out of the breakfast preparations if she was frying eggs for someone like Marcus. There wasn't a woman in the world who could make him happy. She was sure about that. Likely that's why he was still single.

"Anticipating your first Sunday in church?" Lavina asked, glancing up from the bacon pan.

"Oh, very much," Mary assured her. "I hope I pass inspection."

Lavina chuckled. "Everyone will love you, as Leon and I already do. The school board did an excellent job in selecting a teacher for the new term."

"You are very kind." Mary ducked her head.

"Did you and Marcus get along okay on Friday? Dare I ask?"

"He was there when I arrived," Mary said, cloaking the irritation in her voice. She was beginning to feel like she'd been hired primarily to date Marcus. Why couldn't anyone ask about her teaching plans or her goals for the students, rather than harping on Marcus? She set the egg pan on the stovetop to concentrate on turning up the flame.

Lavina clucked her tongue. "He'll get used to having you around soon enough."

"I suppose he has reasons for his disapproval."

"Are you sure the man doesn't fancy you? He really has such a soft heart." Lavina looked hopefully in Mary's direction.

Mary forced herself to nod, but couldn't come up with an appropriate response.

Lavina busied herself with the bacon, stirring the pieces. "There's Leon now," she said with a smile as the outside door opened in the lower stairwell.

Leon's jolly face peered up the stairs. "What do I smell a-cookin'?" he teased.

"Just the usual," Lavina told him.

"The usual is perfect, dear." He grinned and headed into the basement.

"You are such a lovely couple," Mary told Lavina, to the sounds of water splashing in the sink below. "I feel so blessed to board at your house."

A pleased look filled Lavina's face. "Yah, I know. The Lord has given Leon and I many happy years together, but we are the ones who are honored to have you."

Mary didn't protest, allowing the happiness of the moment to sweep over her. This was not so very different from home, but somehow it was new, and exactly what she needed for a fresh start. Maybe after a year of teaching in the community she would be ready to settle down with a husband of her own, someone that fitted her perfectly. Someone she could respect and honor.

A thrill ran up Mary's back. She had never been at this place before, considering a man seriously, even if he was fictional at this point. Truly this was a new day. She had indeed followed the Lord's leading correctly in her move south.

Leon's footsteps came up the basement stairs, and he appeared, his beard still moist from the washing at the sink.

"*Goot* morning," he said officially, pulling out a kitchen chair and sitting down. "What a beautiful Lord's day we have on our hands."

"That it is," Lavina agreed, transferring the bacon and toast to the table. "I think we're ready."

Mary turned off the flame and moved the egg pan to the back of the stove. She placed the plate of eggs on the table and sat down a moment before Lavina did. Leon had noticed that she had made the eggs, and was trying not to inspect them.

Mary hid her smile, and moved the plate a few inches so he could see better. Relief filled his face, which he quickly wiped away, and he cleared his throat loudly. "Let us pray."

Mary bowed her head for the prayer, and tears stung her eyes. She was so blessed with this home that the Lord had provided, much more than she had dared ask or think that she deserved.

Across the road, Marcus bowed his head for the prayer of thanksgiving at the Yoders' breakfast table. The faces of his siblings, and his Mam's, faded as he closed his eyes and silently mouthed his prayer. "Our Father which art in heaven, blessed be Your name. Thank you for this food that is before us, and for the *goot* night's sleep we have had, and for healthy bodies and minds . . ."

The prayer flowed out of habit while his mind raced. He paused for a moment, and then added, "Please help our new schoolteacher to feel welcome." There was more he wanted to pray, but he wasn't sure exactly what.

Mam and his oldest sister, Wilma, began to pass the food around the table. Mam had a fixed look in her eye, but there was no way she could have known about his prayer for Mary. Even if Mam knew, there was nothing unusual about it. What a horrible situation they would be in if the school board had not found a new teacher. He wanted his younger siblings to be properly educated and to learn the discipline that a good teacher would instill. He had no reason to suspect she would perform her duties poorly.

Marcus flinched when Mam interrupted his thoughts. "I have an announcement to make."

He faced her, but Mam was looking at the others.

"I have already told Marcus," Mam said, "but I wanted everyone to know. There is someone coming to visit us this afternoon."

"Uncle Amos?" Charles, the youngest, chirped.

Mam's smile was crooked. "No, sweetheart, this is someone who will be a special friend of mine. At least, I hope so."

"That's awful mysterious," Wilma said.

Esther, the sister born between Wilma and Henry, stared at Mam. "Are you dating someone?"

"Surely not!" Wilma exclaimed.

"Please don't be so shocked," Mam begged. "It is a date, yah, but I shouldn't have waited this long. I haven't been fair to Marcus, or to the rest of you, leaving our home without a dat."

"We were doing just fine," Wilma said, leaping up from the table. She gave Mam an angry look and then stomped away, not giving her a chance to explain.

Mam appeared ready to rush after her, but must have changed her mind. "I . . . I really am sorry for the shock, but this has come suddenly even for me. I guess I just wasn't facing things."

"Who is he?" Mose asked.

"John Beachy," Mam said, "but remember, this is just a date. We don't know yet where it will lead."

Marcus concentrated on his food. Mam was going to marry John Beachy, likely this fall already. Neither of them was young, and as Mam had told him, John Beachy had been trying to win her affections for some time.

"The time has come to move on," Mam said, and left to comfort Wilma.

Marcus ate slowly, the silence heavy around the table.

"Where does this leave you?" Mose finally asked.

"What does that mean?" Marcus retorted.

"There won't be enough work on John's farm for two grown men."

"I suppose not," Marcus allowed. Mose was right. John would surely move into their home and sell his own, much smaller farm to work on theirs.

"Maybe you should be scheduling your own date," Mose said.

"What is a date?" Charles piped up.

"I'll let someone else explain that," Marcus told him, gulping down the last bite of his food. He stood and left for the upstairs. If a new man was moving into the house, it was time for him to find a wife and settle down in a new home. Perhaps he should have felt relieved, but instead he just felt tired. The thought of running around with the other youths, most of whom were much younger than him at this point, did not excite him. *Rumspringa* began at age sixteen for most youths. Marcus was twenty-one, and the role he'd taken on for his family made him feel even older. Well, he'd have to trust that the Lord had a plan for him, even if at the moment it felt like God was leaving him high and dry.

CHAPTER 6

ON THE WAY TO CHURCH, MARY RODE IN THE BACK OF THE Hochstetlers' buggy, with Leon and Lavina seated in the front. The steady clip-clop of their horse's hooves filled her ears. The familiar sound was a great comfort to her continued nervousness. Mary kept checking the road ahead of them, and the home where the services would be held soon appeared. Mary leaned out of the buggy door for a better look. The white two-story structure with its accompanying massive red barn had a string of buggies in the driveway, with more parked in the field behind the barn. The women were unloading their children and moving them up the walks toward the house. Black shawls flapped in the morning breeze, while children clung to their mothers' arms.

"This is Robert Troyer's place," Lavina turned around to say. "They have one child in school, I think."

Mary's mind raced over the list of school children Susie had given her on Friday. "Enos. First grade," she said with a smile.

"Yah!" Lavina was clearly impressed. "Enos will be in school this year. Missy and Robert couldn't have children for a few years. Enos is their first gift from the Lord. They've had two more since then, a girl and a boy."

"One of our most successful farmers," Leon added.

"That he is," Lavina agreed, and turned around in her seat.

"Whoa," Leon called out, bringing Brownie to a lumbering halt at the end of the sidewalk.

Mary followed Lavina out of the buggy and clutched her shawl.

"I see the unmarried men are watching us," Lavina teased as they headed towards the house.

Mary didn't glance over at the line of men who stood near the barn. She did not want to appear as if she was checking them out. The services would begin soon enough, when she would get a proper look at the bench of unmarried men. Her heart was not exactly pounding in anticipation.

"Wouldn't surprise me if you get a few requests for dates by the end of the day," Lavina continued.

Mary gave Lavina another smile but didn't answer. In a way, Lavina's words warmed her heart, and so would the requests for dates from the men, even if she turned them down. She was honest enough to admit that much. There was no shame in finding the attention of men reassuring. The Lord had not yet opened her heart to the love of a man, so she would continue to wait until that special moment arrived.

Lavina opened the front door and they walked in to find a long line of women greeting each other in the living room. Little children moved about underfoot, but everyone was well behaved and staying close to their mothers. Playtime would be after the services ended.

"*Goot* morning," Lavina greeted the first woman in line, and made the introductions. "Mary, our new schoolteacher."

They moved slowly around the circle, shaking hands.

Most of the women added a hug to their greeting, but asked only the basic questions. "When did you arrive? How did you travel down?"

Further details would be shared later around the dinner table, or while she helped serve in the kitchen. As the women gave their names, Mary matched them with the list Susie had given her and made a special effort to memorize the names of each child she encountered. Knowing their names on the first day of school would make an excellent impression. Lucille, the wife of the chairman of the board, Elmer Miller, who Mary had already met, made a point of greeting her with a big smile and a long hug. "Welcome to the community."

"Thank you. It is lovely here."

"I'm glad to hear you saying that. Elmer and I will be down Monday morning to see that you have everything you need. Perhaps help you open your first day? If that's okay?"

"That would be awesome," Mary assured Lucille.

There was also light teasing from the women. "Is Lavina taking care of you? Have you lost weight from her cooking?"

Lavina played along good-naturedly, making faces and acting horrified. Their quiet laughter warmed Mary's heart, and joy filled her. When they completed the full circle, she took her place at the end of the line with Lavina by her side.

"That went *goot*," Lavina whispered in her ear.

Mary nodded, satisfied with the initial reaction from the community.

Outside the house, standing near the barn door, Marcus jumped when a sharp elbow jabbed him in the ribs. "You've been staring at that front door for the last ten minutes. Are you asking the new schoolteacher for a date tonight?"

"I was not staring," he retorted, but the laughter from several men belied his denial. His cousin Emmanuel had made sure his whisper was heard by those who surrounded them.

"She sure is cute," Jonas Esh commented. "I didn't know schoolteachers came that pretty."

"Are you having second thoughts about your wedding this fall?" Emmanuel teased.

Jonas chuckled. "Not a chance, but I speak the truth. Seems like Marcus has been supplied his manna from heaven. No wonder he waited this long."

Marcus didn't respond. They wouldn't believe his protests. He was not about to run Mary's reputation down by mentioning shimmering suitcases. In fact, that bit of information might enhance Mary's standing with most of the men. It was not often that Amish girls came with such flair.

"He's so gone," Emmanuel declared. "Look at the daze he's in."

The laugher rippled down the line.

"Did you hear that Marcus drove the new schoolteacher home from the bus station?" someone added.

"Looks like we were cut out of the action before it began." Emmanuel acted offended. "That's not fair."

"Marcus deserves a chance on this one," someone said. "Don't you think?"

The comment was greeted with more laughter, as the line of men began to move towards the house. Marcus hung back from the still-chuckling men. Bishop Mullet led the way towards the house, his head bowed. The kidding and laughter faded.

Marcus tried to turn his thoughts towards the upcoming sermons, and what the Lord might speak to his heart, but the vision of Mary walking beside Lavina as they moved towards the house wouldn't go away. Even with Mary's bonnet pulled low over her forehead, and her black shawl tight around her shoulders, Mary's beauty had been evident to everyone. Cousin Emmanuel had been correct. He had been staring at the front door long after Mary and Lavina had disappeared inside.

The women had already taken their seats, and Mary kept her eyes on the floor while the men entered the house. They filed in and sat down across from the women's benches. Mary waited until the ministers had left for their usual Sunday morning meeting upstairs before she snuck a glance at the men's section of the room. There were a dozen or so seated on the singles bench. A burly young farmer met her glance and grinned. Mary managed a weak smile in return. He was probably decent and hardworking, and would make some woman very happy, but that woman wasn't her.

Mary put her head down again, but noticed the girl seated beside her smiling across the room. Love was clearly in the air this morning, but she could wait. There was great happiness in teaching school, and she was content.

Mary focused on the songbook and joined in the singing with her whole heart.

Marcus's gaze drifted over to where Mary was seated in the women's section. The ministers had been upstairs for their Sunday morning meeting for over twenty minutes. He had resisted a glance in Mary's direction for what seemed like hours.

Mary had her gaze fixed on the songbook, but her beauty beamed back at him. He blinked twice. Mary had a lingering smile on her face, as if she had been looking at someone, which hadn't been him. So Mary was indeed giving her attentions to some man from the community. He shouldn't care. That was how things should be progressing. Still—Marcus glanced sideways quickly, to see which of the men still wore a ghost of a smile.

Cousin Emmanuel clearly did. He didn't have his head down either, but was boldly looking in Mary's direction. Wasn't he a bit young for Mary? Marcus took a deep breath. He shouldn't be surprised after Emmanuel's teasing out by the barn this morning. Those words must have been a cover for Emmanuel's own interest. Well, more power to the man. Another man had once again beaten him to a woman's heart. He hadn't been trying this time, but the pain still stung, even if Mary was unsuited for him.

Marcus returned his attentions to the songbook and focused on the words. No one said that life made sense. Dat's passing should have shown him that.

Across the room, Mary felt Marcus's gaze linger on her. She had been lost in the song until she became conscious of his gaze.

Should she look up and give him a glare? Let Marcus know that his opinions were not welcome? What was the man criticizing her about this morning? The way she sang? Perhaps how she held the songbook? Or the color of her dress, which was probably too bold for him? Any number of things, no doubt.

Mary waited until Marcus looked away before she lifted her gaze again. She studied his face out of the corner of her eye. He was, without doubt, the most handsome man on the unmarried men's bench. That was the infuriating thing about Marcus. Critical men should be ugly, but this one wasn't.

Mary's gaze drifted down the bench of men. Why didn't the Lord allow her heart to open towards a man? None of the men sitting beside Marcus impressed her, which raised the question, what would a suitable man for her look like? Mary didn't know. She had never seen one. It was like waiting for lightning to strike, but wasn't that how love arrived? She didn't know for certain. Her sisters back home appeared to have made their choices for perfectly practical reasons, but there was more to their choices than they admitted. The glow of love in her sisters' eyes had betrayed that fact.

"He'll be such a *goot* provider for our family," Esther had declared the first time Levi had taken her home on a date.

"I just fit him, that's all," Lois had said about her outing.

Phoebe had done a little better. "Albert is the most handsome man in the community. Why shouldn't I date him?"

Only Albert really wasn't that handsome, so where did the stars in Phoebe's eyes come from? There was more to love than a handsome man. By that standard, her heart should be beating at a rapid pace this morning.

Mary settled her gaze back on her songbook. If Marcus's character matched his good looks, she might be tempted, but she knew better. Who knew what demands and expectations Marcus would lay on a wife? Well, she would not be the one to find out.

Marcus kept his eyes on his songbook until the line of ministers returned from their morning meeting upstairs. The singing stopped mid-stanza once they were seated, and Bishop Mullet stood for the first sermon.

"Dearly beloved," Bishop Mullet began, "join me this beautiful morning in praise and thanksgiving to our great Redeemer and Savior Jesus Christ. We are saved, washed with His precious blood, and called to a life of obedience to His will. Let our minds stir with thoughts of His sufferings on the cross, and the great sacrifice he made in coming to live and walk amongst us."

Marcus listened as the sermon continued. He glanced briefly at Mary again, who was also intently listening. That was good behavior for the community's new schoolteacher, but here he was critiquing her again. Why did he care about Mary's behavior? He hoped Cousin Emmanuel took Mary on a date tonight. Maybe he could stop thinking about her once the woman climbed into another man's buggy.

CHAPTER 7

On Monday morning, Mary wiped the last breakfast dish dry. Lavina stood beside her, having just pulled the plug on the soapy dishwater. A mini vortex formed at the bottom of the sink, and Mary stood transfixed, the dish towel loose in her hand. The water's antics going down the drain had fascinated her since childhood.

"You really should have gone to the schoolhouse ten minutes ago," Lavina told her, with a worried look.

Mary smiled. "I'm on time, and I wanted to help with the dishes."

She waited as the last of the water disappeared.

"Always the schoolteacher," Lavina observed, with an understanding look.

"I hope." A thrill ran up Mary's back. She was a two-year veteran of school teaching, and yet she felt as excited as she had on her very first day of teaching back home.

Leon looked up from his cup of coffee at the kitchen table. "We wish you the best. May the Lord grant you great grace."

"Oh, He will," Mary replied. "But you can pray for me just the same, if you think of it."

"We certainly will," they said together as she grabbed her satchel waiting by the front door to dash outside.

In spite of Lavina's worries, the hour was still early. She had wanted to spend quality time with the old couple who had opened their home to her. This would be her morning routine, following the same pattern, and yet she knew the days would shift with the seasons. On the walk to the schoolhouse, there would be beautiful fall sunrises, like the one currently painted in the sky, followed by cloudy mornings, when rain would threaten, and perhaps even early morning thunderstorms when an umbrella would be needed. The snow would fly eventually, arriving with a brisk cold, which would invigorate the mind. Snowflakes would drift down through the air. There would be still mornings when the white fallen crystals lay thick, the roads yet unplowed. Her boots would crunch in the snow, the world a white expanse of stillness, broken by the distant snort of a horse hitched to an Amish buggy out early on the roads.

Mary's thoughts broke from her reverie when the Yoders' barn door swung open in the distance. Marcus's lengthy frame appeared. He paused when he caught sight of her. Marcus pushed his hat back and stared. Did the man not know that she could see him? The least he could do was wave, or better yet enjoy the beautiful sunrise, instead of gawking in her direction.

Not a single man from the community had requested a date from her on Sunday. Not even Emmanuel Esh, who had made a point of speaking with her after the church service. She supposed that the whole community was conspiring to set Marcus up with her, despite the fact that he didn't like her one bit. It was rather irritating. Not that she would have accepted a date, but to have the possibility removed altogether wasn't quite fair. Even the chairman of the school board was in on this scheme to match her up with Marcus. Why else had Elmer asked him to pick her up at the bus station?

Well! They would have to learn otherwise. Marcus might be the community's favorite son, but they were clearly not the right match. If Marcus wasn't going to make this clear to the others, she would have to.

Marcus was waving now, and Mary limply lifted her hand. She concentrated on the sunrise. The Lord was with her, and had written His encouragement large in the sky this morning. Mary kept her head high and marched on towards the schoolhouse. She reached for the knob when she arrived, to find the door unlocked. Inside, a wave of warmth from the woodstove swept over Mary. Who had lit the fire in the stove?

Marcus must have come early to make sure the place was warm before she arrived. He was the janitor, but she hadn't expected this level of service. Back home she had lit the kindling in the stove herself. Was this what she could expect every morning? Surely Marcus wasn't doing this in an attempt to win her affections? She shook the thought from her head. Clearly, her affections were the last thing on Marcus's mind. He was just a hardworking man, the way everyone said he was. Well, good for him. People were complicated, she thought. It was entirely possible for a man to be good-looking and hardworking while still being obnoxiously critical and arrogant.

Across the fields, Marcus strolled through the barn to finish his chores. He had been up to the schoolhouse well before dawn, since he didn't know Mary's schedule. The last thing he had wanted was for Mary to assume he would time his duties with her appearance each school day morning. He would treat Mary no differently than he had Susie last year, and the year before that. Susie had figured out his schedule, even if she rarely saw him, and thanked him often on Sunday afternoons when they passed each other in the yard after the services. Mary wouldn't be thanking him, but that was okay.

Mary was different from Susie in so many ways. He had made a big mistake when he picked Mary up at the bus station. But maybe things wouldn't have gone much better between them if he hadn't. What would have happened if he had seen Mary at church yesterday for the first time, without the knowledge he had gained on that buggy ride? What conclusions would he have drawn? Where would his heart have gone if he had not known about Mary's shimmering suitcase and flighty, annoying ways?

He might have asked her for a real date. What a mess that would have been. Mary might have accepted his offer, since she wouldn't have known anything about him, either. He would have driven her home from Robert Troyer's place on Sunday evening, instead of from the bus station the week before. Soon enough he would have discovered her materialistic ways and arrogant questioning of everything. What a mess that would have been, to break up with the community's pretty new school-teacher. No one would have blamed Mary, and he wouldn't have either, but the explanations people would have wanted from him would have done great damage to everyone. Mary might make some man happy, but he wouldn't be saddled with a woman who demanded all the finest things and who flaunted her finery to the community. He had been raised to appreciate modesty and contentment in a woman, characteristics that were decidedly absent from Mary.

Better that things turned out this way! How like the Lord to work out good things, even from a man's mistakes. Marcus tried to whistle a tune, a merry little jingle that danced in his head. Where had he heard that song?

Mose stuck his head out of a horse stall to grumble, "What are you so cheerful about this early in the morning?"

"Nothing," he muttered, and cut the whistle mid-jingle. The unfinished part darted and banged around in his head, and begged for expression.

Mose peered suspiciously down the hallway, towards the barn door. "Did you just come from that way?"

Marcus didn't answer, continuing onward.

Mose snorted. "The man just saw Mary."

In a way, but not like you think, he almost said, but Mose wouldn't believe him.

An hour later, Mary stood at the schoolhouse door, ready to greet the first buggy. She had heard the steady clip-clop in the distance. The horse appeared a moment later, trotting along with its head held high. She waved, expecting the buggy door to slide open and the faces of several of her students to appear as they waved back at her.

Instead, Elmer opened the door and shouted, "*Goot* morning, Mary. The Lord has given us a blessed day, indeed."

"Yah, He has," Mary hollered back, walking happily towards the buggy.

Lucille opened her arms when Mary arrived at the buggy, and gave her a hug. "We're here, and you are looking *goot* this morning."

"I'm ready for the school day to start," Mary chirped.

Elmer offered his hand in greeting. "I hope things are still going well for you."

"Yah, certainly." Mary shook his hand. "Thanks so much for coming out this morning. Lucille said you would come, but I had not expected you to arrive before anyone else did."

"It's the least we can do." Elmer grabbed the bridle of his horse. "I'll tie him up and be right inside."

With Lucille by her side, Mary led the way back to the schoolhouse.

"So how are things going at Lavina's place?" Lucille inquired.

"Awesome. It couldn't be better."

"You're happy then?"

"So far," Mary chuckled. "I didn't meet everyone yesterday, but I'm sure the children are well brought up. The community is lovely."

Lucille nodded. "It is. Did you perhaps receive a special invitation yesterday evening? Elmer and I were so happy when Marcus agreed to pick you up at the bus station."

Mary struggled to speak. She was sure these people were well-meaning, but my goodness, they were relentless!

Lucille smiled, obviously drawing the wrong conclusion. "Marcus isn't very open to girls, so you can count yourself privileged indeed."

"There was no special invitation." Mary got the words out. "But Marcus's gesture of driving me home from the bus station was an honor."

"So, nothing happened last evening? What is wrong with that man?"

"I do not think we are well suited for each other," Mary managed, determined to be as blunt as possible and put a stop to this nonsense.

Lucille smiled. "You'll have to be patient with Marcus. Or was he rude?"

"Oh, nothing like that."

Lucille patted Mary's arm. "Things will work then, I'm sure, and here's Elmer now." Lucille turned to greet her husband as they entered the schoolhouse. "Looks like Mary has the place ready to go."

Elmer was looking around. "I think she does, but we expected that of Mary. She came with very high recommendations."

Mary blushed and turned away. Another buggy had pulled into the schoolyard. "Looks like my first students are here." Mary hurried outside. Elmer and Lucille followed more slowly, to remain at the doorstep while she crossed the yard to greet the arriving children.

"*Goot* morning, Gerald." She helped the youngest down the buggy step. "How are you doing this fine morning?"

"*Goot*," he said, smiling shyly up at her.

"And how are you doing?" Mary turned her attentions to the two older girls who had climbed down from the buggy.

"We're doing great," Laura, the older one, answered for both of them. "Sarah and I have been looking forward to the start of a new school year. My last, of course."

Mary gave them both a hug. "I am so glad that I have the honor of teaching your last year of school. Let me help you unhitch the buggy."

They didn't object, while Gerald ran off towards the schoolhouse, his lunch bucket in his hand.

"Gerald wants to get on the softball field quickly," Sarah offered in explanation. "He loves softball. Do you play?"

Mary unfastened a tug before she answered. "I'll be out on the field each day that I can. I don't often hit home runs, but I enjoy the game."

Happy smiles filled their faces.

"Same here," Laura told her, "but Gerald has been looking forward to his first year of school the whole summer, and especially playing softball."

"We'll have to make this a happy year for him, then."

"You are very pretty." Sarah peered up at her. "Even more so than you were on Sunday."

Mary laughed. "And so are you. Shall we go up to the schoolhouse?"

Sarah nodded and retrieved her lunch pail from the buggy. They walked hand in hand up the slight incline, while Laura went to leave their horse in the small barn behind the schoolhouse.

Marcus drove his wagon team out of the back barn door to begin his day's work in the fields. He couldn't resist a glance towards the schoolhouse. There was Elmer's buggy in the yard, which wasn't a surprise. Elmer was the kind of hands-on chairman who would attend a new teacher's first day of school. Susie hadn't warranted that level of attention, but Susie had grown up in the community and knew everyone before she started teaching.

Marcus hung on to the team's reins. There was Mary walking toward the schoolhouse, holding a young girl's hand. They appeared deep in conversation and were laughing together. He could tell from the way Mary threw back her head. A warm circle grew around his heart, quite unexpectedly, but Marcus squashed the emotion. Mary was the community's schoolteacher, and that was the end of the story when it came to his affections. The Lord had allowed him to see Mary's unsuitability on the way home from the bus station. If the Lord had not been gracious towards him, how would he know to resist the woman's charms?

"Thank you," he whispered toward heaven, but he felt awful inside.

Why was the most beautiful girl he had ever laid eyes on not for him? Dat's passing was apparently only the first sorrow which the Lord saw fit to lay upon his heart.

CHAPTER 8

LATER THAT DAY, MARY STOOD BEHIND HOME PLATE AS BETH, ONE OF her sixth-graders, positioned herself on the pitcher's mound and prepared to send the softball towards home plate. Happy voices filled the playground, even when everyone knew there wouldn't be time for a proper game in fifteen minutes. This was practice for the younger students while Laura and the other eighth-grader, Lamar, gathered near second base to choose sides for their lunch-hour game. The whole school was into softball, including the chairman of the board. Elmer had opened classes with a brief morning devotions at nine, and stayed for the first recess period.

"Take a tight grip," Elmer instructed young Gerald. "Keep your eye on that ball, and swing the bat hard."

Gerald appeared intent, his small hands tightly wrapped on the bat.

"This brings back memories of my own school years," Lucille said, standing at Mary's elbow. "School was such a learning experience for me, and fun at the same time."

Mary nodded, and kept her eye on Gerald. He leaned back as the pitch came towards him and swung vigorously. There was a solid whack, and the ball flew high towards second base.

"Run, run!" Elmer hollered to Gerald.

The boy propelled his small body towards first base, his knees pumping high. With all the yelling, Lamar paused from picking his next team member and took a few steps forward to catch the fly.

Elmer was waving his arms at Gerald, who had slowed down. "Run, run! Don't stop!"

Dale, another of the sixth-graders, guarded first, and easily caught the toss from Lamar.

"Out!" Dale declared.

In obedience to Elmer's instructions, Gerald still raced across first base, and Dale stepped aside to let him pass.

"Good job, good job." Elmer poured on the praise. "That was a great hit for a first-grader."

Gerald beamed with joy upon his return to the home plate area. Elmer slapped him on the back, while Mary opened her arms and gave him a hug.

"That was *goot*," she told him.

"You are great with the children," Lucille whispered in her ear afterward. "I can see that the school board made an excellent choice."

"Thanks." Mary ducked her head.

She didn't deserve the praise, even if things were going well. This was the Lord's doing, and not her own.

Ezra, a fifth-grader, was up to bat, and Elmer was cheering him on.

Ezra hit a grounder and made the run to first base.

"Teacher's turn," someone hollered.

"I can wait," Mary protested.

But Elmer held the bat high, with a big grin on his face. "I think the teacher should bat."

"Okay." Mary gave in. She took her place at the plate, and Beth prepared to pitch.

The ball floated gently into the air, traveling towards home plate. Mary focused. She had done this a hundred times at home, and softball was still softball even in a new community. She swung and the whack felt solid. The ball sailed high into the air, and she was off running, without keeping track of the progress. That was the way to play softball. From the yelled instructions on the field, things would be close. Ahead of her, Dale had his glove outstretched, but the ball had not yet arrived.

She raced across the base before the ball thudded into Dale's glove, and a cheer went up. "Teacher made it!"

"Nice play!" Dale complimented her. Mary bent over on first base, trying to catch her breath.

Beth was ready to pitch again, when Mary remembered. "I have to ring the bell."

Dale groaned. "So soon? Can't we have a few more minutes?"

Mary gave him a smile, but didn't bother to answer. Rules could be ignored later in the year, but not on the first day of school.

Mary left first base and headed inside. The clock on the wall read 10:44. There was a minute to spare. Mary pulled on the bell rope to send the loud clangs across the schoolyard. She returned to the door, watching the students race back towards the schoolhouse.

Elmer and Lucille came as far as the door, where Elmer extended his hand. "The Lord's blessings to you. We have been privileged to spend time with you this morning. That was a great ball game."

"Thanks for coming," Mary told him

Lucille leaned close and whispered, "I'll be praying for your school teaching."

Mary braced herself for yet another comment about Marcus, but mercifully there wasn't one. *Phew.* Perhaps she had managed to set Lucille straight on that matter after all. She entered the schoolhouse to find everyone in their seats. A few students were already busy with their paperwork, the others just settling in.

"Sixth-grade reading class," she announced, and Beth and Dale grabbed their papers to head towards the front.

When she arrived at her desk, Mary pulled out the teacher's chair to swivel closer to Beth and Dale, who were seated across from each other on the benches.

Mary took the time to praise Beth. "That was great pitching."

"Yah, it was," Dale added, and Beth's pretty face blushed bright red.

The two glanced at each other quickly, and Beth's embarrassment increased. Obviously, Dale and Beth were sweet on each other. Oh, the wonders of falling in love in the sixth grade.

"Open your books," Mary told them, and the reading began.

Marcus let his team rest at the end of the field, his eyes fixed on the empty schoolyard. Not moments before, the playground had been filled with school children, his five siblings among them, getting ready for a softball game. The faint whack of the bat connecting with the ball had drifted across the fields. Hearing the sound, he had brought his team to a halt at the end of the row. Mary had stood at home plate, directing the action. She had also taken a turn at batting, and had made a great hit. He had not expected that of her. He had a difficult time imagining a girl who owned a shimmering suitcase swinging bats, or racing around bases in a softball game. But Mary had been doing exactly that. He had watched in wonder. She was an odd one, that's for sure.

Marcus broke himself out of his reverie to slap the team's reins and holler, "Time to go. Get up."

They lumbered forward, two stout Belgians who leaned willingly into the traces. Mose operated the second plow at the other end of the field and waved towards him as if to cheer him on with his fruitless fascination with Mary. The plow sliced the ground beneath Marcus, cutting into the earth with a soft hum of sound. He could usually drive the plow the whole day with nothing but peace in his heart, but today he felt restless and disturbed. Memories of his schooldays rushed through his mind, vague images of softball games played in the coolness of the early fall, and even in the cold of winter. He hadn't thought about softball for a long time. Life had seemed too serious for such lighthearted memories. The days when he had held a bat in his hands were a distant memory. Now he had to think like a man, about his duty and responsibilities, about work from sunset to sundown. There was something soothing in hard labor, a settling down of the sharp agony in his heart that wanted to rear its head, even after these long years since Dat had left for glory.

Apparently the Lord had needed Dat more than his family had needed him. That was the only thing that made sense, but even that explanation didn't heal the hurt completely. Mam was also still in pain, but was moving on. After her date with John Beachy yesterday afternoon, the man had stayed for supper. That bode well for the couple's future. Mam planned to wed the man. He could tell from the look of determination on her face this morning.

Mam would not be unhappy with John Beachy. He was kindhearted enough, but he wasn't Dat. Nothing could change that. Mam was forcing Marcus to make his own decisions, which was partly intended, he supposed. He just wasn't going to make the ones Mam wanted him to make. There was no woman in the community he wished to date. Mam had surprised him the other evening by saying she wanted to sell the farm, and she hoped he would buy it. John wanted to continue to live on his own farm, so if things continued as planned, she would move in with him, along with the younger children, after the marriage. Although Mam didn't state it explicitly, she hoped he would find a wife to settle on the family farm with him.

There was another option that hadn't been discussed. Marcus could buy the farm and live there by himself, but it was a lonely proposition after he had borne the load of his family's care for so many years. Did the Lord have something against him? Here he was, single, with no prospects of dating, and about to have a farm on his hands. He would have to square his shoulders and bear the hand life dealt him. Bitterness against the Lord's ways was never right, no matter how difficult those ways were to understand.

As the end of the field came up, Marcus pulled back on the reins. He expertly lifted the plow out of the ground and turned the team around. The soft thud of their hooves and the hum of the plow settled around him again, but peace did not come. The vision of Mary running towards first base danced in his head and wouldn't go away.

By five o'clock that evening, Mary finished checking the day's papers, and rose from her chair to stretch both arms high into the air.

"My, what a day!" she exclaimed as a great happiness filled her heart.

The students had been so well behaved, and the time Elmer and Lucille had spent with her in the morning had been such a blessing. She was sure they approved of her school teaching. Not that she doubted herself, but reassurance was always a comfort to the heart.

Mary gathered up her satchel and banked the fire in the stove. With the warm day, there hadn't been a need to add further wood to the fire since lunchtime. A few coals still glowed among the ashes. Did Marcus stop by in the evenings to check on things? He was mysterious about his comings and goings. She would have to insist on better communication when she saw him next.

For now she would assume that the responsibility to close down the place lay with the teacher. That had been the method used in her prior school. Marcus probably figured she was a babe lost in the woods, and knew nothing about stoves and gas lanterns.

Mary made a face at the schoolhouse door. The man knew little about her. Through the windows she had seen Marcus and his brother Mose working in the fields, but the teams had left for the Yoders' barn moments ago. She was glad of that. With the classes in session, she hadn't thought about the close proximity of Marcus's critical eye, but when she walked home, Marcus could see her across the open fields. There was no sense in enduring more of the man's negative opinions. She was sure he was thinking plenty of them. She wondered if Marcus saw her hit that fly ball during the first recess, and if he had watched her race towards first base with her dress flying. She hadn't felt anything but approval from Elmer or Lucille, who had been standing right there. Why should she worry about what Marcus thought of a schoolteacher who threw herself into a softball game?

Mary locked the schoolhouse door behind her. Well, she wouldn't worry. That was that. Who was Marcus Yoder that his opinion on how she played mattered? He likely thought her undignified and unwomanly. Mary stared down at her dress, disheveled after the ball game and the day of school teaching. Oh well, she couldn't please everyone. She raised her head in the air and marched down the road towards Leon and Lavina's home.

When the Yoders' supper had been eaten that evening, Marcus crossed the fields in the darkness and unlocked the schoolhouse door. He used his flashlight to check the stove and found the fire properly banked. There was no lantern on the ceiling hook, so he checked the closet. The light sat in its proper place, with the air handle tightly closed.

He went into the basement, but nothing was out of place. The ping pong table hadn't been used today, so everyone must have played softball outside. He couldn't remember Susie being able to lure all the students out onto the ball field, but Susie wasn't Mary. The woman must have charmed the whole schoolhouse.

Marcus went back up the steps and closed the schoolhouse door behind him. He walked slowly across the fields, the lights twinkling at him from Leon and Lavina's home. He wished the Lord would send him a woman he could admire and respect and love. Mam would need an answer about the farm soon, but uncertainty filled his heart. Living there alone seemed awfully hard, but neither did he wish to see the place sold to a stranger. Why hadn't God provided him with a good woman to be his companion and partner? Well, he would not complain, but accept what the Lord gave with a broken and humble spirit. That was the way of the community, and the way of the Lord.

CHAPTER 9

MARY OPENED THE SCHOOLHOUSE DOOR ON THURSDAY MORNING with a smile on her face. In spite of a few students' having headaches yesterday, things were going fairly smoothly through this first week. The headaches had been handled in stride. She had been authorized to dispense Ibuprofen, and had found some in the closet medicine cabinet, along with bandages and tape, which Mary hoped would never be needed. Blood was not something she handled well. She might end up on the floor beside the injured student—unconscious. The parents would likely sympathize with a teacher who fainted, but why tempt fate. Better to run a well-organized school where injuries didn't happen.

There were two days left in the teaching week. On Saturday, she would catch up on her school papers and prepare the lessons for the following week. Sunday would be a much needed day of rest, when she would listen to the sermons and receive the spiritual nourishment she needed.

Mary closed the schoolhouse door slowly behind her. She wanted to linger, but clouds had gathered in the sky, as she knew they would, and rain threatened. There had been no repeat of the glorious sunrise that hung in the sky on Monday morning. From the looks of things, the children would have to forgo their beloved softball game today and play in the basement. The same might be true for tomorrow if the ball field remained wet. Well, that couldn't be helped. She didn't want muddy boots tracking through the whole place, and worse, for her students to return home with mud-smeared pant legs and dresses bespattered with the muck from the playground. Better to face the students' grumbling and keep them inside. The mothers of the community would understand the frustration of pent-up young people better than extra dirty wash on Monday morning.

Mary went up the inside steps and was greeted with the usual warmth from the stove. Marcus had been here, as he had been each morning. He must slip away moments before she came down the road from the Hochstetlers' home, she realized.

Why had such a man been placed in her life? She didn't object to the presence of decent men, but Marcus was beyond the pale. Perhaps the Lord had placed this trial in her life to purify her for the love of a real man. Once married, she would look back at Marcus's criticisms with thankfulness in her heart for the pain his disapproval had brought her. In the meantime, she shouldn't be bothered by the man, but in spite of her best resolutions, she was. Possibly because it seemed like everywhere she went, someone was reminding her what a good, hardworking, handsome, *available* man he was. Was she the only one who had seen his faults?

Mary walked over to the window and waved at the first buggy that had pulled into the driveway. Another one followed close behind. Laura and Beth hopped out. Laura busied herself unhitching, while Beth took the time to wave back. Beth was such a cheerful girl, not unlike herself. She had to resist the temptation of having a teacher's pet. With Beth, that would be a struggle. The Lord had blessed Mary with a schoolhouse full of lovely students, but some were lovelier than others—that's just how it was.

Mary went to open the front door and waved towards the road when Lavina's buggy went past, headed into West Union for a day of shopping.

"Send up a little prayer for me," Lavina had requested of Leon at the breakfast table. "You know I've never enjoyed driving into town by myself."

Leon had nodded, and silently added an extra line when they bowed their heads in thanksgiving before the meal.

Mary closed her eyes for a second, and whispered a quick prayer. "Be with Lavina today, Lord. Keep her safe."

Mary opened her eyes to see Beth running up the incline, her lunch bucket flying. Mary opened her arms for the girl and pulled her close. "How are you this morning, sweetheart?"

"Okay." Beth beamed up at Mary. "Laura got another headache on the way to school."

"Oh. I'm sorry to hear that."

"Mam wanted Laura to stay home," Beth said, "but Laura thought she could make it through the day."

"Well, that's a brave girl." Mary patted Beth on the back. "Run inside while I greet the others."

Beth ran off, waving over her shoulder and disappearing into the schoolhouse. Mary glanced towards the heavens. The clouds overhead appeared thicker than they had when she had walked up earlier from the Hochstetlers' home. Maybe the rain would hold off until the students had arrived and were inside. More buggies were coming into the driveway, so no one would be late, from the looks of things.

Mary met Laura coming out of the small barn. "How're you doing?"

Laura tried to smile. "I'm here."

"Are you sure you shouldn't have stayed home?"

"Mam said there is a flu going around, but so far it's been just headaches." Laura shrugged. "I believe we have more Ibuprofen in the medicine cabinet. I'll live. I don't want to miss a day's school the first week. Those are the hardest to catch up with."

"That's wise, I guess." Mary smiled. "We'll try to keep it a peaceful day then. What with the rain we'll probably stay inside."

Laura made a face. "Sorry for the others, but I won't be playing softball, that's for sure. Rain or no rain."

"Go inside then, and I'll be in soon."

Laura moved off, her fingers pressing her forehead briefly.

"Help us today, Lord." Mary sent the prayer heavenward before she turned to meet the next student with a smile and a cheerful, "*Goot* morning!"

Marcus paused after he swung the forkful of stall muck towards the wagon. Mose was working beside him and had stopped to lean on his fork.

"You okay?" Marcus inquired.

Mose didn't answer, his head hung low.

Marcus waited, his eye on his brother.

"Headache," Mose finally muttered. "Splitting headache since breakfast."

"You seemed to eat well enough." Marcus tried for a light-hearted tone. Mose's face appeared haggard. "Maybe you should take a short break."

Mose nodded and sat down on a nearby hay bale. Marcus stuck his fork in the muck again and heaved upward. The plunk of the load landing in the wagon was almost drowned out by Mose's violent choking noises. Marcus whirled about to see his brother bent double, vomiting on the concrete floor, with both hands clutched on his stomach. Marcus dropped the fork to rush over.

"Mose. What happened?"

"Threw up," his brother said, stating the obvious, followed by another violent propulsion of Mose's breakfast onto the barn floor.

Marcus wasn't usually squeamish about people throwing up, but Mose's face had turned nearly green and he was shaking, and the concern for his brother made Marcus feel almost lightheaded.

"You should go into the house." Marcus's voice was gentle but decisive.

Mose looked up in horror.

"Yah, you're sick," Marcus insisted.

"It's the middle of the morning!"

"You're sick."

Mose's objection was wiped away by another heave of his stomach.

"Come." Marcus laid his hand on his brother's shoulders.

Mose stood and staggered a few steps. Marcus stayed with him until they reached the barn door and Mose was headed across the lawn.

Marcus's gaze drifted over to the schoolhouse. A light rain had begun to fall and the view was clouded across the fields. Mary would be busy with her morning classes by now. His younger sister had been sick the day before, and Marcus suspected it was a flu going around the community. Should he warn Mary?

Marcus frowned and closed the barn door. The flu could well be limited to his family at this point. Mary didn't want him involved in her school teaching. He could already feel her silent disapproval of his janitorial schedule. He would go no further. Mary was capable of taking care of herself. If not, she could ask for help. As the janitor, he was willing to help where needed, but he would not humiliate himself by showing up at the schoolhouse door on the vague chance that a flu bug had spread beyond his family and was about to rear its furious head in the community. Mary would think he counted her incapable of handling the routine duties of school teaching.

Marcus reached for the fork again and plunged the prongs into the muck. He heaved, and threw the load towards the wagon.

"First-grade arithmetic," Mary called out, and tried to ignore the noises coming from the girls' bathroom. Laura had rushed inside right after their brief morning devotions and hadn't returned. She was obviously throwing up. Should she knock on the bathroom door? Perhaps not. That might embarrass Laura more than help.

Mary forced a smile as the shuffle of small feet hurried up front and the children situated themselves on the two benches she used for classes. She shifted her gaze to them and tried to concentrate.

"Let's see," she began. "We learned the first of our numbers yesterday. Can anyone tell me what they were?"

"One and two," little Enos piped up.

"That's right." Mary gave him an encouraging smile. "Can you write the number one on the blackboard?"

Enos nodded his head vigorously and jumped to his feet. There were more violent noises coming from the girls' bathroom, but Enos didn't seem to hear them. He proudly drew the number one on the blackboard.

"That's perfect," Mary told him. "Erase the number and take your seat." She stood to her feet. "Just give me a minute."

Several of the students sat at their desks with their faces turned towards the girls' bathroom. Mary hurried past them and knocked on the bathroom door. "Are you okay?"

An unintelligible answer came back.

"Can you open, please?"

Another muffled croak.

This was serious. "Laura, please open."

The lock turned, and the door cracked.

"Are you okay?"

Laura's pale face nodded, but she didn't open the door further.

"Can I help?"

"I'll be out in a minute."

Mary hesitated. "Okay, but I'm here if you need anything."

"I know." Laura closed the door again, and the lock clicked in place.

Mary turned back towards the first-grade class seated on the benches up front. She froze at the sight before her. Little Gerald was bent double, his hands clutched on his stomach and a stream of his breakfast spread out on the hardwood floor, with a portion smeared on little Bonnie's dress. Shock was written over Bonnie's face. The tears would clearly burst in a second.

Mary forced herself to move forward, in spite of the room moving sideways. The puddle on the floor stared up at her, the edges creeping ever wider. She clutched the back of a student's desk as her knees went weak, and the world slowly went dark.

Marcus was working diligently in the stall when the barn door creaked behind him. He turned to see Mam enter the musty building.

"How is Mose?" Marcus asked, throwing another forkful of muck towards the wagon.

"He'll be okay. It's the others I'm concerned about. Mary might have her hands full today."

"Mary. Does she have the flu?"

"Not Mary," Mam said. "I sent Henry and Ronda off with headaches this morning. They didn't want to stay home on their first week of school, with a new teacher in the schoolhouse. I thought they had a touch of the cold, but nothing serious. Now, with Mose so sick, I'm afraid I was wrong. I'm walking over to the schoolhouse to check on them."

"I can go."

Mam shook her head. "You have enough to do."

Marcus followed Mam to the barn door and watched her walk across the fields. He wanted to go, but hadn't dared insist. Mam was right. He had to let go of things. He had plenty on his plate.

CHAPTER 10

Mary regained consciousness on the schoolhouse floor to find a soft pillow under her head. Someone was rubbing her forehead with a wet cloth. Mary groaned and forced open her eyes. The face of Marcus's mam, Silvia, came into focus.

Mary's arms flailed as she tried to sit.

Silvia clucked her tongue. "Take it easy, dear. You must have struck your head on the way down."

"I fainted?" Horror gripped Mary, and she made it upright this time. Her head throbbed, and a fog hung on the edges of the schoolhouse ceiling.

"Are you okay?" Silvia asked. "Let me help you back to your chair."

Mary clung to Silvia's arms and hobbled over to her desk. The benches were empty of the first-graders, but the stream of vomit still lay on the floor. The memories came back in a rush. She had been in the midst of the first-grade arithmetic class when she had gone to help Laura in the bathroom, and returned . . .

Mary groaned and settled into her chair. "Where is everybody?"

"They are here," Silvia assured her. "I sent someone down to Lavina for help."

"Lavina!" Mary jumped to her feet, and everything threatened to fade again. She promptly sat down again. "Lavina is in town shopping."

"When did she go?"

"Earlier this morning. About the time the school children were arriving."

"I see," Silvia said. "That's why I must have missed her buggy leaving. I'll send for help from Marcus instead."

"Marcus!" Mary cried.

"Yah, Marcus," Silvia said. "I can help you with the schoolhouse, but he'll have to take Laura home. Beth can't drive the buggy by herself."

Mary wilted into her chair. She would never live down this disgrace. Fainting over the sight of vomit, and now Marcus was coming. The throbbing in her head became worse.

"Can I do anything for you?" Silvia asked.

"Maybe Ibuprofen," Mary suggested.

Silvia left, and Mary focused on her schoolroom. The students sat in their seats with stunned expressions on their faces. Laura was not among them.

When Silvia returned with the Ibuprofen bottle and a glass of water, Mary asked, "How did you know to come over?"

Silvia wrinkled her forehead. "I'm afraid I have a confession to make. I sent Henry and Rhoda to school this morning with headaches. I thought they had a cold, but apparently that's the first sign of this nasty flu, and it gets much worse after that. Mose is quite sick at home. I'm sorry this is happening."

Mary swallowed two Ibuprofen and stood to her feet. "I think I'm the one to blame in this situation."

Silvia patted Mary's arm. "Don't talk like that. The flu is so different every year. This one seems to strike fast, once it gets going."

"What do we do now?" Mary racked her brain for answers. There was vomit on her schoolhouse floor, and several students appeared ready to add their own.

"We should clean up," Silvia said. "Marcus will be here in a moment."

Mary moved towards the washroom, where she knew there were buckets and mops.

Silvia stopped her with a touch on the arm. "I'll go. You just had a nasty fall."

Mary shook her head. "Watch the children. This is my problem."

Perhaps if she cleaned the floor without throwing up, she could redeem some of her dignity. She should be on her hands and knees, hard at work when Marcus arrived. The news of her fainting would at least be muted in his critical mind.

Marcus had the wagon filled with muck when the barn door burst open.

His oldest sister, Wilma, rushed inside, her face flushed. "You have to come to the schoolhouse at once."

Marcus froze.

"Mary fainted," Wilma said, "and half the school is sick."

"Mary!" Concern rippled through him. To cover up, he said loudly, "Half the school? That's not possible."

"Maybe not," Wilma allowed. "But it seemed like it when Gerald threw up in front of the schoolhouse and Mary fainted. Regardless, Mam wants you to come and drive Laura and Beth home. Laura is quite sick."

"How is Mary?" Marcus asked, setting his fork as calmly as he could against the wall.

"It was awful!" Wilma declared. "I never saw a teacher faint before. I tried to help her, but she was still unconscious when Mam arrived."

"Unconscious?" He couldn't hide his alarm.

Wilma noticed. "She's not dead."

Marcus took a deep breath. "Good thing Mam went up."

"I know." Wilma was looking skeptically at him. "Are you going to help, or faint yourself?"

"Let's go then," he muttered.

Wilma tagged along behind him as Marcus tried not to run across the fields.

"How hard did she fall?" Marcus asked over his shoulder.

"I don't know. She just fainted away right in the middle of the room."

"Like fell over? Crashed down?"

"Not like that," Wilma said. "She went down slowly."

"How long was she out?"

"A little while until Mam came."

"Can she walk around now?"

"I don't know. She was sitting in her chair when I left. Mam sent Esther down to fetch Lavina, but Mary told her Lavina was in town. That's when Mam sent me to get you."

They had arrived at the schoolhouse, and Marcus slowed down to enter quietly. Mam met him at the top of stairs. "You need to get Laura and Beth's horse ready and drive them home."

"Where's Mary?" he asked, looking around.

Mam motioned towards the front of the schoolhouse. Marcus stepped around her for a better look. She was on her hands and knees, wiping the floor with a washcloth. Mary had to have heard him enter, but she didn't look up.

"Is she okay?" he asked.

"I'll take care of things," Mam told him.

Marcus didn't move. "I should help clean up."

"Just go," Mam said. "We'll take care of it. Check on Mose when you get home, and someone needs to come pick up the other sick children."

Marcus forced himself to walk away and had the horse hitched to the buggy by the time Mam helped Laura out of the schoolhouse, with Beth holding her hand. Marcus waited until the sisters had climbed in before he joined them and jiggled the reins to drive out of the schoolyard.

Mary held her breath as she wiped the cracks in the hardwood floor one last time. The Lysol in the water helped the smell. There had been no choice but to get down on her hands and knees after she had cleaned up what she could with the mop. In the background Mary had heard the hurried whispers between Marcus and Silvia. She had almost passed out a second time from the shame of what Marcus must be thinking. At least she had been working when he arrived. Never in her wildest dreams had she expected something like this to happen during the first week of classes.

Mary stood slowly to her feet and dropped the washcloth into the bucket. Silvia was coming back up the stairs after leading Laura and Beth outside, and Mary met her halfway across the floor.

Silvia held out her hand and took the bucket. "I'll stay a minute longer until you wash up in the bathroom."

Mary's head spun as she steadied herself and arrived at the bathroom without mishap. She cleaned her hands thoroughly with soap and warm water. The smell of the vomit still hung in her memory, but the traces were gone from her fingers. Mary shivered. Maybe the scent of the soap masked the smell, which would return with a vengeance in the middle of the school day? She would faint away again. She couldn't close school in her first week of classes, even if now many of the children had gone home sick.

Mary gathered her courage and left the bathroom. Silvia was keeping her eye on the remaining school children, with the bucket of water on the floor beside her. "Be back in a minute," Silvia mouthed, and left for the basement.

Mary forced herself to walk to the front and face the classroom. "I . . . I know I fainted," she began. No one laughed. "I'm sorry about that. I don't normally faint, but today has been a strange day, so let's see if we can put the pieces together. First thing, if anyone else feels the slightest bit ill, you had better go home."

Mary held her breath. She half hoped everyone would go home, though she'd never admit it.

"I don't want you to leave, but if you're ill you should."

No one left, and Mary forced herself to smile. "Okay. We'll try to continue now. Let's have our first recess while we calm our nerves. With the rain, we'd better stay inside and play in the basement. We don't need muddy clothes on top of the tale you will have to tell your parents tonight."

There were faint smiles on some of the girls' faces, but no one laughed. They stood and traipsed down to the basement. Mary fell into her chair, but didn't dare hold her head. The Ibuprofen hadn't taken hold yet.

Footsteps came across the schoolhouse floor, and Mary looked up.

"Are you okay?" Silvia asked.

"I am," Mary assured her.

"Is there anything I can do to help?"

Teach school for the day, Mary almost said.

Silvia was waiting.

"I'll be fine in a minute. After I get over my embarrassment."

"That could have happened to anyone," Silvia comforted her.

"Thanks for saying so." Mary stood. "I'll send for help if I need any."

"I'll have Marcus come over after school hours to check on you."

Mary didn't have the energy to protest.

"I'll be going then," Silvia said, and left.

Mary watched them walk across the fields from the schoolhouse door and stifled a groan as her headache stabbed painfully. She would not faint again. She also would not finish the school day a minute early. She simply wouldn't.

Marcus couldn't stop thinking about Mary and how she was managing. He was tempted to walk over and ask, foolish as that would appear. The work of janitors was limited, and didn't include checking in on schoolteachers during class time.

Mam informed him at lunchtime, "I told Mary you would be up to see her after school let out."

He kept his eagerness from showing, and simply nodded. The hours dragged on, and Marcus's concern increased at the last recess hour when none of the children came outside to play. The rain had stopped, but maybe it was too wet to play softball. When the last buggy pulled out of the driveway, he hurried across the fields. This had been a rough day for Mary, for this to happen in the first week of her new school term. She might be vain and materialistic, but Mary didn't deserve this.

He removed his boots outside the schoolhouse door and entered to find Mary seated at her desk. Marcus cleared his throat.

She looked up with a frown. "Yah."

"Mam said I should come over and see how you are doing?"

"I'm doing okay." Her voice croaked.

He moved up the steps. "You don't sound well."

"I'm fine."

"What happened was not your fault."

The tears shimmered in her eyes. "Says who?"

"It wasn't," he said. "That could have happened to anyone."

Mary made a face. "Fainting at the sight of vomit? I think not. I am to blame."

"You might have a touch of flu yourself. That's why you fainted."

He could see hope rising into her face. "Do you think so?"

"I do," he said. "Let me ask Susie if she would substitute for you tomorrow."

"I can't do that."

"Why not?"

"It's my first week of teaching in a new community."

"So?"

"I can't. That's that."

"Mary, this is a bad flu. Mose has been in bed all day. You should go take care of yourself." The concern in his voice was obvious now, and Mary paused and looked at him for a moment before responding.

"I am weak, but with a few cups of tea tonight, and a good night's sleep, I'll be okay." She pressed her lips together.

He realized pressuring her further would be fruitless. He moved back a step. "I'm sorry you had a rough day. It really wasn't your fault."

She looked up at him with new softness in her eyes. "Thank you for saying so. I'll leave soon. I'll be back early in the morning. You don't have to start the fire."

"I am starting the fire," he said.

She wavered for a moment. "Maybe that would be for the best."

He wanted to linger, but he couldn't think of a good excuse to stay. "You take care," he said, and retreated towards the door.

Mary had her head in her hands when he glanced back over his shoulder. He wanted to comfort her, but what could he do? He had said everything he could say. Marcus hurried out the door, but stopped short when Elmer's buggy came driving in the schoolhouse lane. Elmer was likely here to comfort Mary and offer his sympathy. He shouldn't stay. Marcus waved to Elmer and headed across the fields.

Mary met Elmer at the schoolhouse door with a forced smile on her face.

"How are you?" Elmer inquired.

"Okay. It was an awful day, and I'm sorry."

"Don't beat yourself up," he said kindly. "But I'm afraid I have more bad news."

Mary hung on to the schoolhouse door with both hands.

"I have consulted with several of the other families, and we have decided to call off school tomorrow. We think that might help break the flu cycle over the weekend."

"You would close school tomorrow?" Mary croaked.

"I'm sorry. I know this is happening on your first week of teaching, but it's really not your fault."

She pressed back the tears.

"You get some rest over the weekend," he said. "I'm sure a day off will be the best for everyone."

Mary hung on to the door as Elmer's buggy drove out of the schoolhouse lane. It was several minutes before she found the strength to stagger back to her chair and fall into it.

CHAPTER 11

M ARY ARRIVED AT ROBERT TROYER'S HOME THAT SUNDAY MORNING again, riding in the back of the Hochstetlers' buggy. As Leon drove in the lane, Mary kept the buggy door shut this time. She had no desire to see the line of men standing beside the barn and looking their way sooner than necessary.

Mary was sure thoughts would be buzzing through their minds. Things like, *That's our new schoolteacher who fainted, and she had to close classes during her first week on the job. What a disgrace!*

Marcus had been kind enough on Thursday evening when he walked up to the schoolhouse to check on her, but surely he would blame her for having to close school.

Mary held back the tears, blinking rapidly behind the buggy door.

In the front seat, Lavina was saying to Leon, "There's a lot of men missing. This flu has gotten to everyone."

Lavina was trying to encourage her, so Mary cracked open the buggy door for a look. Lavina was correct. The line was much shorter than usual. Lavina had been certain that nobody from the community would think ill of her for what had happened, and here was proof. If grown men succumbed to this flu bug, she might survive unscathed after the debacle at the schoolhouse on Thursday.

"I should have stayed home myself," Leon muttered in the front seat.

Lavina gave him a worried look. "You were fit as a fiddle when you woke up this morning."

"I know." Leon glanced at Lavina with a twinkle in his eye.

Lavina slapped him playfully on the shoulder. "You're teasing. Well, don't. An old woman like me can't take it."

Leon and Lavina's continued kindness overwhelmed Mary. She had nothing to fear from the parents this morning. The flu wasn't her fault, and yet . . . it was hard not to blame herself.

Mam's letter this past week hadn't helped. "We are struggling with an awful flu up here," Mam had written. "I pray the Lord gives us grace and protection. Several of the older people had to stay home last week from the Sunday services. So far we have managed without closing the school, although a quarter or so of the students were missing."

Mary wondered if she'd brought the flu bug with her, sickening the whole community with her presence.

Leon brought the buggy to a halt at the end of the sidewalk, and Mary climbed out. Wild thoughts raced through her head. Was she feeling ill? She had waited on Friday and Saturday, expecting the illness to strike. Nothing had happened. Was the flu waiting to maximize her humiliation? What a horror if Lavina had to drive her home during the church service. She might throw up in the crowded farmhouse bathroom, or worse, during the sermon in the middle of the seated women.

Mary steadied herself against the morning breeze, not looking at the line of men, as Leon drove the buggy towards the barn. Lavina touched her arm, and together they headed up the sidewalk. Halfway to the front door, Mary couldn't resist and glanced towards the row of men. She couldn't see Marcus standing in the line, but he must be there. Marcus wouldn't succumb to this flu. Marcus probably had never been sick a day of his life.

Lavina paused at the front door to ask, "Are you okay?"

Mary nodded, and they entered the house. Everyone turned towards them, but their faces bore only looks of sympathy. There was no condemnation in sight as several of the women rushed to Mary's side.

"How are you?" they inquired.

"I'm okay."

"Did you come down with the flu?"

"Not yet."

"Be hopeful," one of them said. "You'll probably not catch it."

"It's probably waiting to strike in the middle of next week during classes," Mary moaned, as several of the women chuckled at her morbid humor.

"I'm sorry you have been given such a rough greeting to our community," one of them said.

"I was thinking I probably brought the flu in from the north," Mary replied. "Mam wrote this week that it's raging up there."

"Believe me," someone said, "southern Ohio is quite capable of producing a horrid flu bug of its own."

Everyone laughed as they comforted Mary and seated themselves on the long benches a few minutes before the men filed in. Mary kept her head down until the singing began. She snuck a look at Marcus, who was seated on the unmarried men's bench. He wasn't looking at her, his gaze intent on his songbook.

Mary tried to still her troubled thoughts as the singing continued and the ministers returned from their meeting upstairs. Bishop Mullet rose to his feet and opened the first sermon. "Dearly beloved," the bishop began, "we are blessed of the Lord, as always. Let us give Him the thanksgiving of our hearts, even as life's storms gather on the horizon. We know that the Lord will carry us through every trial and tribulation here on this earth. This morning there are those amongst us who suffer from bodily ailments, but the Lord is still on His throne. This is not, we pray, an illness unto the death." There were chuckles, and the bishop smiled. "We older people can be thankful for the flu shot, and the Lord's grace, of course."

Marcus was smiling at the bishop's joke, but he still hadn't glanced towards her. Just a soft glance would warm her heart and silence the question that tormented her. Did Marcus think she was to blame when the school had to close last week?

Marcus watched Mary out of the corner of his eye while at the same time he listened to Bishop Mullet's sermon. Mary was wearing a light blue Sunday dress, which made her appear even more beautiful than usual, if that was possible. He shouldn't be thinking about Mary's looks with the flu raging through the community. The number of sick folks was high this morning. The Troyers' living room had been overflowing last Sunday. Today, the benches had big gaps between families. Marcus estimated that at least a third of the community was missing.

He couldn't help but wonder if Mary had brought this sickness with her in that shimmering suitcase of hers. That was an awful thing to think, but since Mary's arrival in the community his equilibrium was disturbed. He hadn't blamed Mary for what happened on Thursday. He wasn't beginning to now. Resolutely, Marcus focused on Bishop Mullet's preaching. Mary was not to blame for any of this, he told himself repeatedly.

Mary tried to keep her mind on the preaching, after she snuck a quick look at Marcus. A ghost of a smile lingered on his features, clearly unrelated to anything Bishop Mullet had said. What was Marcus thinking? Did he find mirth in her discomfort and difficulties? He hadn't on Thursday evening.

Mary kept her head down until the service wrapped up a little after twelve. Perhaps Marcus would speak with her when they crossed paths today? Drop some word of reassurance? Even a little smile would help, letting her know that he agreed with everyone else's opinion on the awful events of the week. In the meantime, she would think on the sermon, and gather what comfort she could from the words Bishop Mullet had spoken of the Lord's grace. The Lord's words were better than Marcus's opinion of her. She shouldn't care what the man thought, but she did. Marcus was becoming a grief and a pain. There was no question there.

She ought to challenge him when she spoke with Marcus next. "Why are you always thinking the worse of me, when no one else does?"

He'd of course say, "I'm not."

Which would bring up the turquoise suitcase, if she wanted to press her point. A conversation which had best be left alone. She wouldn't change his mind, no matter what she told him.

Mary slowly stood to her feet along with the other girls and headed towards the kitchen.

"Can I help?" she offered once she arrived.

"Sure," the woman in charge told her. "The unmarried men's table is short-handed today."

"Perfect," she chirped, but the woman missed the irony.

"Sorry about your first week of teaching," the woman said. "That was a horrible introduction to our community."

"I guess things happen," Mary demurred.

The red beet and peanut butter bowls were soon set out, and Bishop Mullet announced the prayer of thanks from the living room. Everyone in the kitchen paused with their heads bowed for a few minutes, until the amen was pronounced.

"The unmarried men's tables are in the basement," the woman directed Mary.

She filled a tray and gingerly took the steps. Another girl was following her, but Mary concentrated on her balance. All she needed was to trip and sail out into the roomful of men, with her red beet and peanut butter bowls flying. That would validate Marcus's opinion of her and surely cast doubt into everyone else's minds, as it rightly should. There was only so much misfortune that could occur before people changed their minds about the most innocent of characters.

"Food, food!" several of the men chanted when she appeared.

Mary completed the steps deftly, and pasted on a bright smile.

"What have we here?" one of the men teased. "Our food delivered at the hand of our pretty new schoolteacher."

Mary lifted her head high, and shot right back, "Don't you wish you were still attending school?"

Their laughter filled the basement.

"Looks like Marcus has his hands full," Marcus's cousin Emmanuel got in edgewise.

Mary ignored the comment and emptied her tray. "There we are. I'll be right back with refills."

"Marcus can't wait," Emmanuel teased.

Mary made a face at him, and the laughter pealed again. Mary caught sight of Marcus seated at the end of the table. He wasn't laughing, and instead looked on the verge of reprimanding the men.

Mary hurried up the stairs, and tripped on the third step. She caught herself on the handrail, and turned quickly. Marcus was looking at her with a concerned expression. At least the man cared whether she broke her leg. She whirled about and sped upward.

Marcus watched Mary's light blue dress disappear up the stairwell. The woman had plenty of courage. He had to grant her that. With what Mary had faced last week, most girls would have stayed in the safe confines of the kitchen today. Instead, Mary had obviously volunteered to serve the men's table. She was a puzzle and a fascination, for sure.

The man seated beside Marcus punched him in the ribs. "She's something, isn't she?"

Marcus grimaced. "After this week, I do have to agree with that opinion."

CHAPTER 12

MARY DROVE LEON AND LAVINA'S BUGGY TO THE YOUNG FOLKS' gathering at Bishop Mullet's home by herself the following Thursday evening. School attendance had been sparse since the first of the week, but the classes had remained open. That was an accomplishment in itself. She had been tense on Sunday evening, expecting Elmer's buggy to drive in the Hochstetlers' lane with news of another school closure on Monday.

Elmer hadn't visited, and a small victory had been gained. Leon and Lavina had rejoiced with her. That hadn't kept Leon from coming down with the flu, though. She had arrived home from the schoolhouse tonight to find the man in bed, with Lavina fussing over him and fixing tea in the kitchen.

"Can I help with anything?" Mary had inquired.

"Just don't get sick yourself," Lavina had told her, making a face. "This is awful stuff."

"What about you? How are you doing?"

"So far, so good. Flu shots." Lavina had attempted a smile. "Some work and some don't, I guess."

Mary pulled back the reins at a stop sign. Leon's horse, Brownie, shook his head in protest, as if he knew someone else was driving. Brownie had never made trouble when Leon drove him to church. Surely the horse wouldn't act up tonight. She could imagine him rearing or balking along the road just about the time Marcus and his brother Mose drove past in their buggy. Marcus would stop to help, but he would also think she ruined everything, including her host's horse.

"Slow boy, slow boy," Mary comforted Brownie. The horse gave a few more shakes of his head, followed by a loud snort. Mary clung to the reins until the road was clear. She let them out slowly. Brownie took off with his head held high, trotting briskly along. Mary kept her eyes on the road and stilled the pounding of her heart. Leon would not have let her leave the Hochstetlers' place driving a dangerous horse. She would just have to keep a firm grip on the reins.

As the miles rolled past under the buggy and Brownie made no further trouble, Mary's thoughts drifted to Marcus. He had stayed out of sight this week, though the stove had been lit each morning when she arrived. Better that Marcus kept his distance until she was on firm footing with her school teaching job again.

Mary bounced into Bishop Mullet's driveway, barely missing the ditch with the left wheel. The buggy tilted crazily as she careened up to the barn. Several young men who were standing in the yard hurried forward to help her unhitch.

"Having a little trouble with Leon's horse?" one of them teased.

"Should I?" she shot back.

"Leon likes to drive half-tamed racehorses." Laughter rose from the men.

Mary pressed her lips together, and didn't answer.

"Leon is very good with horses," the man continued. "I suppose he figured Brownie wouldn't revert back to his old ways."

"I'm surprised Lavina hasn't warned you," another one said.

"So it's that bad?"

They laughed. "Not really. We're teasing."

"So who am I to believe?" Mary glared at them.

They had Brownie out of the shafts by now, and led him towards the barn, chuckling amongst themselves and ignoring her. She was left standing by herself. Before she could leave for the house another buggy pulled in the driveway. Mary caught sight of the faces inside and ducked out of sight, but Marcus and his brother Mose had to have seen her. In which case, she was not about to act as if she had anything to hide.

Mary stepped out of the shadows as their buggy halted beside hers.

"*Goot* evening." Mose leaned out of the buggy to greet her with a big smile.

"*Goot* evening," she replied.

Marcus was climbing out of the other side, but hadn't said anything.

"Are you helping us unhitch?" Mose teased.

"Right!" she snapped. "Two grown men, and they can't unhitch their own horse?"

"Marcus has been sick with the flu bug all week." Mose lowered his voice. "Yet he insisted on coming tonight to see you."

"He did not," Mary retorted.

"Who do you think has been lighting your fires in the morning?" Mose winked. "The man is devoted to you."

Mary stared. "I'm perfectly capable, especially if Marcus is sick."

"What are you two talking about?" Marcus asked from the other side of the buggy.

Mary marched around their horse to face Marcus.

"Why didn't you tell me you were sick this week? I could have lit the stove myself."

He attempted to laugh. "I wasn't that sick."

"And I'm supposed to believe that. This flu is awful. I could have done the fires myself. That's what I'm used to."

"I'm here now, so all is well." Marcus brushed her objections aside.

"How bad was it?" Mary couldn't keep the concern out of her voice.

"He threw up all day Tuesday," Mose hollered from the other side of the horse.

"You didn't. Oh, I'm so sorry."

"Others were sick too," Marcus said.

"I'm still sorry. How are you feeling tonight? You look a little pale."

"I said I'm fine."

"Ready!" Mose hollered, and Marcus turned to hold the shafts while Mose led their horse forward.

"You're serious?" she asked as Mose retreated towards the barn door. "You were sick with the flu, and tending to my schoolhouse?"

"I sent Mose down one morning."

"You are avoiding the point."

"Maybe." He shrugged.

Mary didn't press it. "Next time, please admit you're sick, and I can light the stove myself. I am capable, you know."

"The schoolhouse should be warm by the time the school children get there."

"You don't think I could get there early enough?"

Marcus shrugged.

"I didn't have the least bit of problem in the two years I taught at home, and we were located further north than West Union."

"Maybe no one told you the schoolhouse was cold?"

"They would have complained, believe me."

"I am the janitor here in West Union," he said. "I will do what I think is best."

"Oh, you will!"

"Yah, because I am responsible."

"And I am not!"

"I didn't say that," he said.

Mary didn't respond, turning to march towards the house where a group of girls had gathered on the front porch.

Marcus watched Mary storm up the walks. The woman had her dander up. What had he said that was so wrong? Marcus pressed his forehead with his fingers. He had mostly recovered from the flu, but his head still ached, and now this. He should have stayed home tonight, if that hadn't disagreed with his principles. He was trying to get out more, to participate in youth functions like his mam said he should.

He had also wanted to see Mary again, if he was honest. That thought troubled him the most.

Another buggy rattled in the driveway and Marcus walked over to help his cousin Emmanuel unhitch.

"You are looking a little sober for a man in love," Emmanuel teased.

"Why didn't you take Mary home on Sunday evening?" Marcus retorted.

Emmanuel laughed. "Because I thought you were taking her home."

"I'm not," Marcus grumbled.

Emmanuel was clearly unconvinced. "Wasn't that Mary going into the house right now? Did you have a sweet chat with her?"

Marcus ignored the question. "I've been down with the flu this week."

Emmanuel was undeterred. "So why didn't you take the girl home on Sunday evening?"

"I was down with the flu."

"On Sunday evening?"

"No."

"Then what are you waiting for? The woman is clearly made for you. Wake up, man!"

"You're crazy."

Emmanuel shook his head with a befuddled look on his face, and led his horse towards the barn. Marcus followed, glancing over his shoulder. Mary was deep in conversation with a group of girls on the porch, gesturing, her arms emphasizing some point. Why would Emmanuel say that Mary was well suited for him? There was nothing about the woman suited to him. Not one thing!

An hour later Mary focused on the volleyball that hung high in the sky, headed on its downward arch, straight towards the position she played in. Emmanuel, the team's coach, had assigned Marcus to a place beside her. She hadn't protested or made a fuss when Emmanuel gave the instructions, in spite of the obvious implications intended. Let Marcus deal with his community's misinterpretation of their relationship. She was not to blame.

With the ball coming, she had to make a quick decision. Should she step aside and let Marcus deal with the incoming play? He was recovering from the flu, but that didn't mean much when it came to Marcus Yoder. His tensed body was poised in her side vision, ready to step in if she faltered, which meant that he didn't think her capable of dealing with the ball. She was not going to back down, regardless of his expectations. She wouldn't have done so at home, and she wouldn't do so here, even if she wound up missing the ball.

Mary blocked the thought of Marcus's opinions from her mind. She would go for a full return. No one knew her well enough in the community to cooperate with a setup. Especially Marcus, who anticipated only failure on her part. Mary raised both hands and met the incoming missile. The thud on contact was followed by a clean arch of the ball back over the net.

Mary heard Marcus exhale softly beside her.

She couldn't resist the dig. "Didn't think I could do it?"

"That was pretty good," he said.

"I'll set it up next time," she told him.

Incredulity crossed Marcus's face.

"Just move towards the net when the chance comes," she instructed.

"She's telling you," Emmanuel hollered towards them. "You had better listen."

Marcus appeared to waver.

Emmanuel quipped, "She got that last play, didn't she?"

Mary gave Emmanuel a sweet smile. "Nice to have someone on my side. Thank you."

"I'm always on your side," he said with a grin. "I have to get Cousin Dufus in line."

That wasn't exactly what she had in mind, but Emmanuel was trying to help.

"Ready?" she asked in Marcus's direction.

"I guess," he said, clearly unconvinced.

Marcus snuck a glance in Mary's direction whenever he dared. Her volleyball skills were entirely unexpected. He waited with bated breath when the ball was being served again, but the arch went in a different direction.

Would Mary actually dare set up a ball for him? He couldn't believe her confidence. Few plays were as difficult or effective as the setup where one player purposefully failed to return the ball, bouncing it into an arch near the net instead, where another player would leap up and spike downward. The one who set the ball would need a high level of skill both in judging distance and speed.

Pretty schoolteachers were not up to the task. He was sure about that. Mary would only frustrate and embarrass herself. Marcus opened his mouth to object, but the ball was heading their way again.

"Set," Mary said loudly, so confident.

Marcus willed himself to move into position. He could hardly breathe. He wanted Mary to succeed, and yet she couldn't. She simply couldn't.

He watched the arch of the ball, and Mary jumped high with both hands extended. The return play came toward him, perfectly. He leaped up and pounded downwards. The other team groaned as Marcus threw himself backward to avoid the net and keep his balance at the same time. The ball slammed the ground on the other side of the net, the other team unable to react quickly enough to save it.

"You did that very well," Mary said, her eyes glowing.

"And so did you," he said, returning the compliment.

"We're a good team."

Marcus looked the other way. He was trying to collect his scattered thoughts.

"That'a girl!" Emmanuel hollered towards them.

His cousin didn't sound astonished. Wasn't anyone else shocked by Mary's volleyball-playing abilities?

Mary was still smiling at him, even gloating a little, he was sure. Did she really mean that, about being a good team?

CHAPTER 13

Mary entered the schoolhouse earlier than usual on Monday morning, where silence greeted her. She paused to listen. There were no noises coming from the basement, or from the upper level of the schoolhouse. She had hoped there would be, that she would catch Marcus at his duties.

Mary moved up the steps and the warmth of the stove greeted her. She removed her coat and lingered for a moment with her eyes closed. Marcus had been much more pleasant over the weekend, less critical, perhaps even approving of her. She hadn't imagined the change in his opinion, she was sure. Neither had the volleyball game last week been a dream. They had played so well together. On the one hand, she should be offended with Marcus's continued underestimation of her. On the other hand, perhaps the man had simply never met someone like her.

That was a very prideful thought, but also a delicious one. She had impressed the high standards of Marcus Yoder. She, Mary Wagler, of the turquoise blue suitcase fame! There was sweet irony in even a small victory over the man's high opinions. Deep down she shouldn't care. There was no future for Marcus and her, not in the way the community seemed to think. But the volleyball game had been truly satisfying. The whole youth group had been impressed with how well they played together.

Mary danced a little jig in front of the warm stove. She would savor her accomplishment and the smile Marcus had grudgingly given her during the services yesterday. Before the school year was over, she would make Marcus acknowledge his mistaken evaluation of her on that day they drove home from the bus station. Marcus might never learn to like her, but he would come to see that he had been wrong about her character. Like, *really* wrong.

Perhaps that was part of her mission in this community? To help Marcus? His critical ways and need to control events must come from the early loss of his dat. No one from the community talked much about what had happened, but from bits and pieces of conversation she had picked up, everyone's heart had gone out to the lad left to carry such a heavy burden at a young age. Marcus was admired for having endured the trial, which, thought Mary, was part of the problem. Life was more than endurance. There was joy and happiness, and gladness along the road. She could almost excuse Marcus his harshness, given how he must have suffered from his loss, and doubtless still suffered. But he couldn't wallow in his grief forever, and he certainly shouldn't take out his negative feelings about life on her! Marcus meant to change her. Instead, what was needed was for her to help him grow into the kind of man he should be— kinder, gentler, and more understanding of things which were new to him. Looking at things from that angle, her turquoise blue suitcase was the door into a better world. The poor man. What a shock to his senses. Marcus must never have seen such edgy luggage carried about by a proper Amish woman.

Mary eased herself into the teacher's desk and surveyed the empty classroom. This was her domain, her kingdom, from where she would minister to young hearts, and apparently to a not-so-young heart who lived across the fields. Marcus needed help. How was he to find a girlfriend with that attitude of his? He was handsome and talented enough and there was no reason things couldn't change for him with the right kind of influence. Right then and there, Mary decided the crowning touch of her first year in this community would be to find Marcus a girl-friend, or at least make him presentable to the right kind of girl.

Who knew how many women the man had scared away? She could understand their reactions. What if she had been open to his attentions on that ride home from the bus station, only to have her heart bruised and injured like an open rose after a late frost? The man had no tact or subtlety. Not the least bit.

Mary stood and walked over to the schoolhouse window. The yard was still empty of buggies. There wouldn't be any students for another hour or so. She had plenty of work she could do. There were lessons to go over, the eighth-grade math equations should be studied before she presented the lecture in class, and there was Marcus to think about. She would have to pray for the man. He required some kind, yet firm, guidance. In order for him to heal from his past, she would have to get him to open up about his feelings, which would be no easy task. Yet with the Lord's strength she would do so, and thrive during her first year living here in this community. More had occurred last week at the volleyball game than an excellently executed play.

"Give me wisdom, dear Lord." Mary breathed a quick prayer heavenward and returned to her desk.

A moment later, Marcus slipped through the fence and approached the schoolhouse. He had a weak excuse for another visit this morning, but a poor one was better than none. He pushed open the door and stopped short. Mary was sitting behind her desk, gazing out of the side windows. She appeared deep in thought, and obviously hadn't heard his approach. What should he do now? He was about to startle her, in addition to having to explain why he had returned.

Marcus stepped back and waited. Mary's gaze out of the window was intense. What was she thinking about? Her lessons?

Marcus took a deep breath and cleared his throat. Mary gasped and looked up. "Why are you here?"

He took off his hat and came up the steps. "The wood pile in the basement is a little low," he began. "I'm sure you noticed. There's also none left out by the barn. I've decided to call for a work day on Saturday, for those who can come, and we'll cut wood from our fallen timber in the back forty."

She was staring at him. "I hadn't noticed about the wood."

His hat went around and around in his hand as he grappled for a way to continue the conversation. "How are things going with the classes?"

"It's Monday morning."

"No more flu bug." He tried to laugh.

"I'm trying to wipe that week from my memory."

"You don't have to. Everyone understood," he said.

She turned back to the window. "Maybe? But on to another subject since you are here. Tell me about your dat. You never talk about him."

His hands froze and his whole body stiffened. "My dat? Why?"

"How did he pass?" She was looking intently at him, her big blue eyes like pools of water.

"Heart attack." Where was this coming from? Why did she want to know about his dat?

"Was it expected?"

"They rarely are."

"So there was no warning at all?"

"He always had a weak heart. There was nothing the doctors could do."

"How did it happen?"

He paused, reflecting. Her voice had taken on an unexpected softness, and he found his initial defensiveness melting away. He didn't like being interrogated, but he couldn't quite make himself put an end to it. He felt almost trapped by her presence, but he wasn't entirely sure he wanted to break free.

"He didn't wake up one morning," he answered, looking down at the floor.

For a moment, silence fell in the room. She seemed to be waiting for something from him, but he didn't know what.

Finally she spoke again, her voice gentle, knowing, like she saw right into his soul. "And all that responsibility fell on you."

"Yah," he managed, then quickly added, "But I enjoy farming. It's good for a man to work hard."

"You were much too young, I would think."

That broke the spell. He was so sick of people pitying him, reminding him that the burden he carried was too heavy, as if that made any difference. "I guess you'll have to take that up with the Lord," he said, his voice suddenly harsh. He turned to go. Enough was enough.

"Marcus." She was out of her seat. "I'm not trying to offend you. I'm interested, and I care."

"That doesn't change anything."

Mary could almost see the battle going on inside him. Inexplicably, he turned back toward her and sat down in the closest desk chair.

"Caring always changes things. It makes things easier," she said, as gently as she could, as if she were approaching a wild animal that she didn't wish to scare off.

"The community cared," he said. "That didn't change anything."

"Isn't that an awfully cynical attitude?"

"I really should be going. I don't want to take up your time." But he didn't stand up.

"Marcus, please," she begged. "We should talk about this. Talking helps."

He met her gaze. "I really don't think so. There is still duty which must be done, and precious time is wasted."

"Marcus." She smiled sweetly. "I . . . Tell me about your mam then. She is dating again?"

"She is."

"How do you feel about that?"

"What does it matter how I feel? She's dating, and moving on. It's time, and I should do the same."

"But this must be rough? Having a man to take your dat's place?"

"Mam could have married right away. That was none of my business."

"But she didn't."

He didn't answer.

"Did you object, perhaps, even if it would have made life easier for you?" She came closer and sat in a student's chair.

He stood reflexively, uncomfortably aware of her nearness, but he didn't move to leave. "I don't know what you mean."

"You have to know what I mean. The burden of the farm fell on your shoulders, and your loyalty to your dat, and your mam's love for him, probably made it hard for her to consider another man. Waiting was courageous of both of you."

"I have no idea what you are talking about."

"Come, Marcus. You're intelligent. You don't give yourself the credit you are due."

"Duty and responsibility are requirements of the Lord," he said. "What I did was nothing more than what is the responsibility of any man."

"The loss of your father still had to hurt."

"Of course," he said, "and now I have to go. I'm not complaining." This time he managed to make himself move toward the door. How could he feel so uncomfortable, and yet drawn to her like she held a powerful magnet? Why did it take so much effort to leave?

"Admitting the pain," she called after him. "That's not complaining."

"We accept the Lord's will," he called over his shoulder. "As a teacher, you should know that."

"I do, and I also know that we can become hard and brittle on the inside. That's not *goot*."

He tipped his hat at the schoolhouse door. "You have a *goot* day now. The weather should stay warmer, so I think you have enough wood to last until the weekend."

She had her mouth open to say something more, but he left, not looking back as he rushed across the fields towards home.

Mary hurried to the other side of the schoolhouse and stared through the window at Marcus's retreating back. She had said too much. Way too much, but the words had bubbled out without much thought. She wanted to help the man. In fact, she had decided it was her mission to help him, and his reaction showed plainly that she was right. But she should have moved more slowly, parsed her words. Instead she had barged ahead and probably injured him further. She would have to try again when she saw him next. There were always second chances with the Lord. That was a lesson she had learned a long time ago. Perhaps this had been a start, at least. He had begun to open up, even with her clumsiness, hadn't he? Teaching never was easy. She knew that. The rewards came at the end of a lesson well taught and finally learned.

The sound of buggy wheels driving into the lane came from the other side of the schoolhouse. Mary crossed over for a quick glance out of the window before she went outside. Laura and Beth had their horse out of the shafts by the time she arrived.

"*Goot* morning, girls," Mary greeted them cheerfully.

"*Goot* morning," they chorused.

"Was that Marcus going across the fields?" Laura teased with a sly smile.

"Yah," Mary admitted, a rush of heat filling her face.

"He's a nice man," Beth said, obviously trying to ease Mary's discomfort. "Everyone thinks so."

"That he is," Mary agreed. "Marcus is planning a wood frolic here at the school on Saturday."

Beth and Laura exchanged grins, and Mary's blush grew worse. There was no way she could explain to her students what the conversation between them had been about. That would only make things worse. Beth and Laura would have to go on believing that romance had burned brightly in the schoolhouse.

Mary turned to wave at another buggy coming into the schoolyard, and hurried over to help unhitch. Out of the corner of her eye, Mary noticed that Laura winked at Beth, but that couldn't be helped. Sometimes a helping hand was misunderstood. If Marcus's injured heart could be reached, her humiliation was a small price to pay.

Across the fields, Marcus wandered through the Yoders' barn in a daze. Mose had the team working outside in the fields, otherwise his brother would have a field day teasing him for his confusion. He was smitten, but not in the way Mose would conclude. Mary's nerve continued to confound him. What gave Mary the right to think she could lecture him and the rest of the community on Dat's passing? Their hearts had been broken. That much was the truth. But Mary was wrong in so many other ways, yet so bold in presenting her opinions. He would have to stay away from the schoolhouse for a while, which was not a problem. He could arrive early as he had been doing, and leave well before Mary arrived. So no more excuses for unplanned trips to speak with Mary. He shouldn't have gone over this morning. Why did he keep making mistakes with the woman? His good sense must have left the day Mary arrived.

Marcus focused on his task in the barnyard, but Mary's face filled his mind. The image was bright as the noonday sun, and wouldn't fade. He tried anyway, to no avail. In frustration he paced the barnyard. Why did such beauty abide in a dangerous and misguided woman? The Lord never made mistakes, but this time he, Marcus Yoder, was tempted to doubt.

CHAPTER 14

MARY LEFT THE SCHOOLHOUSE EARLY THAT EVENING, WALKING towards the Hochstetlers' place with her tote bag slung over her shoulders. Usually the weight wasn't too heavy, but tonight the bag was filled with books she needed to study for tomorrow's lessons. She had been unable to concentrate at the schoolhouse since classes had been dismissed. The flood of memories from her conversation with Marcus that morning rushed back in to torment her. Perhaps she could concentrate in her bedroom, away from the spot where she had tried to help Marcus, only to have her bold words hurt the man more than they helped.

As she passed, Mary snuck a glance toward the Yoders' homestead. The cows were gathered in the barnyard, so the evening chores had begun. She should change into an everyday dress and return with an offer to help with the milking. Perhaps a demonstration of her good will would soothe the feelings between them? At the very least, she could try to explain herself further. She only wanted to help, to get Marcus to admit the wound his dat's passing had left so that he could move on, open his heart to some woman, discover joy again.

Did she dare? She had an hour to spare before Lavina expected her home for supper.

Mary hurried towards the Hochstetlers' home and entered the front door. Lavina was not in sight, but there were soft puttering noises coming from the basement. She would explain herself later. She went up the stairs and changed into an everyday dress. Lavina was still not up from the basement when she came down. Out the door she went, and up the Yoders' driveway five minutes later. There was motion in the kitchen window, but no one appeared to question her arrival. Mary slipped through the barn door, which creaked shut behind her. The familiar musty odor of cows and barn stalls rushed over her. She took a moment to draw a deep breath. She missed home more than she had remembered. The pace of the past weeks had left little time to think of her sisters and their families. Their meddling ways seemed distant at the moment, with the sting removed. They had only meant to help her. Somehow, she had always known that deep down.

A form of a man came around the corner, and Mary pasted on a smile. "Hi."

Mose stopped short. "Oh, it's you."

"How are you this evening?" She kept her voice chirpy.

"Okay. And you?"

"Fine. Marcus is planning a wood frolic at the school on Saturday."

"So he told me." Mose pointed towards the interior of the barn. "He's over there, throwing down silage before we milk."

"Thank you." Mary moved past him, led by the steady sound of silage coming down the chute, with hollow thumps as each forkful hit the concrete floor. Mary leaned inward between the landings to peer up the silo slide.

"Marcus."

There was no answer.

She called louder, "Marcus!"

His face appeared far above her in an open silo gate. "Yah."

"It's Mary."

Incredulity filled his face. "Mary! What are you doing here?"

"Can I come up?"

He didn't answer for a moment. "Can you climb a silo?"

She bit back a sharp retort. She hadn't come here to argue with him. "I grew up on a farm," she said, as sweetly as she could.

His head stayed in the silo gate, apparently contemplating her answer.

"I need to speak with you," she encouraged him.

"About what?" His answer echoed in the chute.

"Can we speak up there?" she begged.

"Okay." His head withdrew, as if he didn't wish to witness her climb.

Mary left her tote bag on the floor and grasped the first rung. She pulled herself upward on the wire steps. When she reached the top, his face betrayed relief and, she couldn't help but notice, approval.

"Come in." He stepped closer, looking a bit concerned.

"I don't bite." She extended her hand. "Help me."

His fingers were calloused and strong. They wrapped themselves around hers like a vice, and she was propelled into the main silo hold.

Mary brushed the silage from her dress. "There! I'm here!"

"You are." He still looked surprised by that fact.

"Shall I help?" She reached for the fork he held in his hand.

He didn't move. "You came to help me throw down silage?"

"I don't see another fork." She smiled her brightest.

"Do you even know how?"

"When are you going to stop doubting me? I grew up on a farm, as I said."

"Right. Does your dat milk cows?"

"He used to."

"And you climbed silos?" He studied her intently.

"Why does that surprise you?"

"So you did?"

"We are going in circles."

"We usually do," he said, and smiled a bit.

"I am very sorry about this morning. I really am."

"You are certainly opinionated."

She kept her mouth shut for a moment. "I am sorry for *how* I said what I did, not for what I said."

"What kind of apology is that?"

"A sincere one, and from my heart. I had no right to say those things to you, even if they are true."

A ghost of a smile flickered on his face. "You climbed a silo to tell me that?"

"And to help you." She held out her hand. "My way of saying I'm sorry."

"That's an interesting way," he said, but he did let go of the fork.

She grasped the handle and heaved a load of silage towards the gate. A satisfying thump rumbled up from below. Mary heaved again, and again. The work was difficult, but she was accomplishing the task.

"My turn," he said, and held out his hand.

She stood back while he worked, watching his muscles ripple in his arm. He made it look easy. When he was done, he stood up, leaning on the pitchfork.

"You do know how to throw down silage," he said, smiling.

"It's not rocket science. Yet you doubted me."

"Are you here to quarrel with me again?"

She gave him a sweet smile. "No. Sorry."

"You first." He motioned towards the silo gate.

Mary clambered out, and made sure her dress didn't hang on the sharp metal edges. Marcus waited until she was at the bottom before he began to climb down. Little chips of silage heralded his appearance before his legs came into view. He brushed the debris from his hat and hung the fork on the wall.

"I'd like to help with the milking," she told him.

"Nah, you don't have to help us with the chores."

"But I want to. For tonight."

"Well, I guess I won't turn down help," he said. "Even from the community's schoolteacher. That is, if she insists."

"I insist."

"Then follow me." He led the way back across the barn. They continued through the barn towards the soft lowing of the cattle. Mose had them in their stanchions, with feed spread in the trough. The cows' long tongues licked the delicacies greedily.

"I thought you two got lost back there," Mose commented.

"Mary is helping with the milking tonight," Marcus told his brother.

"Oh. She can milk?" Mose teased. "I didn't think pretty girls could do farm work."

"I am an Amish farm girl," Mary snapped. "Of course I can milk."

"Feisty, are we?" Mose chuckled. "We can use some feistiness around here. No question there. Marcus can be dried up like the summer's hay most of the time."

"The milk pails are over there, and the stools below them." Marcus motioned towards the far wall. "And ignore Mose."

Mose winked at her. "No harm meant. I was teasing."

"I know that." She gave him a gentle smile. "I'd best get busy."

Mary picked up a three-legged stool and sat down beside the nearest cow.

Marcus snuck a quick glance at Mary. Her head was hidden behind the cow's haunches, but by the motions of her hands he could see she knew what she was doing. When would the woman stop surprising him? Maybe he had been wrong about her, even if she did have a sharp tongue. Mary had stopped in after her day of teaching school to help with their chores. This was clearly more than a peace offering. Mary cared about them, and about him. Why, he wasn't sure.

He pulled his gaze away and headed into the milk house. He needed a moment to clear his head. Mary's presence rattled him, as usual, and muddled his thinking. She could be flighty one moment, and a practical Amish farm girl throwing down silage and milking cows the next.

Mose passed him in the aisle with a punch in his ribs, and a loud whisper. "Is that woman something or what? She came to help you chore."

"So what?" Marcus retorted.

Mose leaned closer. "You should be jumping up and down for joy. You are not even dating Mary, and she comes over to help you. What's wrong with you?"

"Mary is a *wunderbah* schoolteacher," Marcus said, and hurried on, leaving Mose in the aisle staring after him.

He washed his face in the cold water at the milk house tank, and ran his fingers through his hair. The chill took the flush out of his face. He could not remember when a woman had affected him like this.

"Get a grip," Marcus muttered, and returned to find Mose milking a cow next to Mary and deep in conversation with her.

"I see you playing softball with the children every day," Mose was saying. "That's what our teacher used to do, but not every day."

"I love softball," Mary said. "I'm not that good at it, but it's fun."

"I think you're great at the game, from what I can see." Mose chuckled. "Maybe not as good as you are at volleyball, but still good."

"Volleyball is fun." Mary ducked her head lower. She had noticed Marcus listening. Marcus grabbed a stool and moved to the far end of the line of cows. He could still hear Mose and Mary's chatter, but he didn't join in. Mary had made a heartfelt gesture with her apology, and was now helping with the chores. Still, the woman was dangerous. He simply knew she was. There was no changing that. With his janitorial duties and the woodcutting coming at the schoolhouse on Saturday, he would have to maintain a professional relationship with Mary, but nothing more. Absolutely nothing more!

CHAPTER 15

A BRIEF RAIN SQUALL HAD MOVED THROUGH THE COMMUNITY EARLY that Saturday morning, leaving a slight wetness on the ground and water clinging to the branches of the bare trees, but nothing to call off the community's planned woodcutting for the school. Mary adjusted her woolen coat and scarf before she filled her arms again with pieces of split firewood. She stood and dumped the load into the wagon. The team of horses belonged to Marcus, a pair of massive Belgians, their coats shiny even in the cloudy weather. They were standing patiently at the moment, waiting for a signal to pull the wagon back to the schoolhouse. She had purposefully chosen to work at Marcus's wagon, waiting for her own moment to speak with him, but so far Marcus had been busy elsewhere. At least he pretended he was. Likely he wanted to avoid her entirely today. Well, the man wouldn't be able to dodge her the whole morning.

Mary filled her arms with wood again. Two more wagon teams worked in the woods, surrounded by men with chainsaws, who were cutting up the fallen timber that the young men had dragged into handy straight lines earlier. The men also had the use of two unattached teams, which could be tied to the tangled logs and hauled apart with shouted commands raised above the roar of the saws.

"Quite a damp morning for this," the girl working beside Mary commented.

"But a perfect day nonetheless. At least we're not sweating."

The girl smiled, agreeing. "We should have quite a stack done by lunchtime."

"This is so *wunderbah*. The community doing this for me."

The girl looked at her strangely. "This is a community event each fall. I'm surprised Marcus didn't schedule the event earlier. I noticed your wood pile behind the barn was almost gone."

"That it was," Mary agreed. "Likely Marcus just was busy."

"Mmhmm." The girl smiled knowingly and filled her arms with wood pieces.

Mary continued to make trips between the cut wood and the wagon. She wanted to protest that she was not a distraction to Marcus, even if the evidence pointed in that direction. Marcus scorned her most of the time, which was about as far as one could get from being in love. Men in love fawned over the objects of their affection, while Marcus couldn't stay far enough away from her. She had hoped the tensions between them would ease after her overture with the Yoders' chores, but Marcus hadn't made an appearance at the schoolhouse for the rest of the week. She would have to keep trying. Her plan was to get him to open up and deal with his pain, and then she would look for a suitable young woman to match him up with. There was no sense playing matchmaker yet, before he was ready to love someone. But how surprised the community would be when Marcus finally asked the right girl for a date, and Mary would have the sweet satisfaction of knowing she'd helped him get to that point!

Mary threw on another armful of wood.

"We about got it loaded," the girl said. "Want to drive Marcus's team up to the schoolhouse?"

Mary caught her breath. "I don't know about that."

"He shouldn't object, and you do know how to drive?"

"Of course."

"You definitely are a match for him." The girl's smile grew. "Shall we go?"

Mary hesitated until one of the men shouted, "Come on! One of you girls take this team. We have our hands full splitting the wood."

"See! Let's go!" the girl whispered.

She was trapped. Mary forced herself to hop up on the wagon bed and grab the reins. The girl followed her, standing by her side, obviously enjoying the moment.

The team perked up their ears at the tension on the reins. "Getup!" Mary hollered in her best teacher's voice.

They lurched forward, and the wagon headed towards the schoolhouse.

"There's a deep ditch going out on the left," the girl warned.

Mary hauled the reins to the right as the team stomped through the fallen branches.

"You're doing fine," the girl encouraged her.

Mary glanced over her shoulder. Was Marcus watching?

"Take it slow now," the girl warned. "We don't want to overturn this load."

Across the section of fallen trees, Marcus wiped the sweat from his brow and set down his saw. Working in the woods was always strenuous, but fun at the same time as the community came together for a common cause. Come lunchtime, there would be a delicious meal served by the older women in the schoolhouse basement. He could already taste the meatloaf casseroles and tossed salads. There would also be pies served by the dozen— cherry, apple, and pecan. No one would go home hungry.

Marcus's pleased smile froze on his face. Who was driving his team towards the schoolhouse? The load of wood bounced in the wagon as the wheels went over fallen branches and the bed tilted sideways.

Two girls were driving, which was not unusual. Everyone helped out where needed on days like this, so he shouldn't be alarmed. The community girls were raised on farms, so they knew how to handle horses, of which his team was among the best behaved. Still, traversing the wood on a day like today was a challenging task.

Marcus looked closer. Mary was driving! He was sure now. The outline of the figure under the coat was clearly Mary's, even if he couldn't see her face.

"Looks like the girl's making herself right at home?" a man's voice teased from across the fallen log.

"Looks like it." Marcus tried to keep the tension out of his voice. Mary thought she could do anything, and so far she usually could, but there were dangers hidden in the woods she knew nothing about.

"Think she can handle the team?" the man asked, pushing back his hat for a better look.

"I'm sure Mary can." Marcus tried to sound confident and reached for his saw. He could pretend he wasn't worried. He was about to pull the starter rope when the man's words stopped him.

"Looks like they got stuck."

Marcus looked up at once. One wheel of the wagon was indeed sunk deep into the ground, and his team of horses was straining at the traces.

"Better go help," the man said, but Marcus had already set down his saw and taken off running across the fallen limbs, dodging sideways, sliding and half falling to the wet ground.

"Pull back on the reins," he hollered when he regained his footing. "Hold back the horses." The instructions were swallowed up in the vastness of the woods and the roar of the chainsaws.

Would Mary have the sense to contain the team? The Belgians' massive strength could easily tear the traces, or break the single tree. He imagined the team of Belgians galloping through the woods without the wagon, with Mary hanging on to the reins in desperation. He would blame himself forever for the accident. He should have stayed with his wagon. Instead he had headed into the woods to keep his distance from Mary. This was what happened when a person shirked his duty, whatever the reason.

"I didn't see the hole!" the girl beside Mary was wailing. "We should never have done this."

Mary hung on to the reins as the Belgians lunged forward again, desperate to proceed after the unexpected stop.

"Let them go," the girl advised. "We can't stay stuck. Not with Marcus's wagon."

"They'll tear the traces," Mary muttered.

"Marcus is coming," the girl moaned. "I'll never live down this shame. We have to get out of this hole."

"The horses can't!" Mary shouted this time.

She didn't know how she knew, but she knew. For one, the wagon bed went clear to the ground on the right side, and the weight of the wood load had shifted that way. A single tree took only so much pressure before it snapped. Permanent damage would happen then, the kind of damage she didn't want to contemplate. She would never let go of the reins if that happened. Getting the wagon stuck wasn't totally her fault, but having Marcus's team tangle themselves around a fallen branch or, worse, a standing tree would be on her hands.

"Let them pull," the girl begged. "We can get out of this before Marcus arrives."

Mary sawed back on the reins instead. "Easy, boys. Easy, boys," she said, attempting to soothe the Belgians.

Out of the corner of her eye, Mary saw several men run towards them and head straight for the horses' heads. She held on until they grasped the bridles and pushed the heaving Belgians backward.

"Are you okay?" one of them called to the girls.

"I think so," Mary called back, trying to catch her breath.

"We're so sorry about this," the girl whimpered beside her.

"Could have happened to anyone," someone told her.

More men arrived and appraised the situation. "We have to prop up the wheel before we try to drive forward," one of them said.

Another man had hopped up on the wagon and held out his hand. "Shall I take the reins?"

"Certainly." Mary handed them over.

"You did real well in holding back the horses when that wheel went down," the man said. "Could have torn loose from the wagon otherwise."

Mary jumped to the ground with her heart pounding. After the tension, tears stung her eyes at the man's praise. The girl who had ridden with her fled. Mary dug out her handkerchief and wiped her eyes. When she could see, Marcus was standing in front of her.

Mary's mouth worked silently, but no words came out.

"It's okay. It's okay," Marcus heard himself say repeatedly. Around him men rushed to aid the stricken wagon. Two of them held the bridles of his Belgians, while others inserted fallen timbers under the main beam.

He should join the rescue effort, but he couldn't move. Mary was crying, and the sight tied his heart in knots.

"I'm sorry about this," he said. "I should have been here to drive my team. It's okay, really."

She stared up at him silently.

"You did well. You really did," he added. "Not every girl would have known to contain the team."

Mary really began crying.

"I'm so sorry," he said. "Did I say the wrong thing?"

"No," she sobbed.

"Then why are you crying? You did *goot*."

"That's why I'm crying."

Mary was making no sense at all.

She didn't say anything more, wiping her eyes and watching the bustle as the men raised one end of the wagon into the air. They filled the hole with pieces of wood, and slowly the wheel was lowered to the ground.

"Let the horses go," the man at the reins was instructed.

The wagon lurched forward and the rear wheel bounced over the filled hole without hanging up. A cheer went up from the men.

"I should go help unload," Mary said, breaking into Marcus's daze.

She was moving away, and he reached for her hand without thinking and brushed her fingers. "I'll see you later."

Mary nodded, before she rushed away. He stared after her. What had he just done? Mary hadn't appeared offended, but never had he taken such liberties with a girl. The instinct to comfort her had overpowered him.

Marcus continued to watch her retreating figure until Mary reached the wagon parked behind the barn. She began to unload the wood, and didn't look back. He forced himself to turn away and return to his saw sitting on the ground where he had left it beside the fallen log.

CHAPTER 16

AT LUNCHTIME, MARY STOOD IN LINE AT THE SERVING TABLE SET UP in the schoolhouse basement. An array of casseroles, salads, bread, butter, and fresh jam were spread out before her. Fresh-squeezed lemonade sat in a bucket at the end with pies lined up on an adjacent table for dessert. Through the window Mary could see the immense pile of wood behind the barn, which the community's efforts had produced that morning. Saws were set in neat lines nearby, with discarded coats thrown over the wood pile. Soft, cheerful conversations rose and fell around her.

Mary caught sight of Marcus seated on the far side of the room. He had been through the other side of the table moments earlier. She had lingered, not wanting to abide the awkward moments when they would fill their plates across from each other at the serving table. Marcus obviously regretted the brief moment of endearment that had passed between them. The gesture could not have been an accident. Her hand still tingled from the light touch of Marcus's fingers after the team and wagon had been rescued from the hole in the woods. Marcus had clearly tried to comfort her. But then he had been studiously ignoring her ever since he had come in from the woods for dinner.

She wished now she had expressed more emotion, perhaps with a quick squeeze of her hand in response, instead of rushing off towards the schoolhouse, but his compassion had caught her so off guard. Marcus had seemed to genuinely care about her accident. His concern had gone deeper than any potential damage to the wagon or his team of horses. The worried look in his eyes had been about her.

Mary forced herself to breathe. William and Sarah, the parents of one of her students, were filling their plates across from her.

"Quite a *goot* morning of work that was." William glanced over at her and grinned.

"Yah, it was," Mary agreed.

Sarah chimed in, "I wanted to tell you, our Josiah so enjoys your classes. He can't stop talking about school when he gets home."

"Thank you," Mary replied sweetly. Now she was embarrassed. "If I only knew how to drive a wagon in the woods."

"Oh, that." William dismissively waved his hand. "The woods are full of holes, and you handled Marcus's team quite well. He is greatly blessed of the Lord, I would say." William's grin grew.

"Thank you," Mary managed.

Protesting her relationship with Marcus was useless. She was certain several people had witnessed his expression of endearment, and word spread quickly.

"Not only is Marcus blessed." Sarah beamed across the table at her. "You have been such a blessing to everyone in the short time you have been in our community. Our prayers for a new schoolteacher have been abundantly answered, as have Marcus's prayers, I'm sure. We wish you both the Lord's greatest blessings."

"That we do," William echoed.

Mary nearly dumped a spoonful of casserole on the table instead of onto her plate, but William and Sarah didn't appear to notice.

William was pointing to one of the meat casseroles, commenting to Sarah, "This looks delicious."

"Yah! Pricilla, Bishop Mullet's wife, made that," Sarah replied.

William appeared satisfied and dished several spoonfuls onto his plate. Mary steadied her hand as she filled her glass with lemonade at the end of the table and took a sip to calm her nerves. She glanced around for a place to sit, and saw Marcus motioning for her to cross the room and sit beside him. She froze. Had she been wrong about him again? Had Marcus not been ignoring her? Goodness, he was confusing.

Marcus motioned again, more emphatically this time. She could ignore him, and no one would notice in this chattering crowd. But she didn't want to. That was the perplexing truth. Marcus should not have such power over her with a simple touch of his hand. Maybe the excitement of the day had affected her? Her feelings would likely settle down after she ate lunch. She forced her feet to move in Marcus's direction, dodging several small children who raced across the crowded room.

Marcus made room for her beside him on the bench. Several people noticed and sent sly, approving smiles their way. Well, they would have to think what they wished. She was not dating the man, and didn't plan to. Marcus would never ask her for a date, even if she wanted him to. Which she didn't!

"There." Mary sat down. "Why are you asking me to sit beside you?"

He grinned. "The food is delicious."

"I suppose so." She took a bite and avoided his gaze.

"The pile of wood behind the barn is pretty high," he said.

"It is," she agreed. "That should last me for this winter and leave enough for next year's schoolteacher."

His spoon froze in midair. "You're leaving after this term?"

She didn't look at him. "Maybe? I have yet to think about next year. It's a little early."

His spoon moved again. "Everyone is very appreciative of your teaching. You should stay."

"You think so?"

"My siblings love your teaching. I've never heard so much chatter about all the things they're learning. And the parents obviously approve of you, too."

"I'm a first-term teacher and a new girl in the community."

"You have clearly impressed everyone," he said.

She took a bite of the meat casserole. "Except you?"

"You were quite *goot* with my team this morning," he said.

She let his dodge pass. "Well, I am glad I came to the community. I think the Lord was definitely leading."

"That seems to be the general feeling."

Mary ate slowly and didn't respond.

"Mam is marrying next month," he finally said. "Middle of November, it looks like."

"That's *wunderbah*."

"It is time," he said.

"Did you know this was coming?"

"Not really, but I should have expected it, I guess."

She paused before replying. She didn't want to mess things up this time. Neither did she want to pass up this opportunity for a meaningful conversation.

She kept her voice as gentle as she could. "How do you feel about your life changing so much again?"

"I don't know what that means."

"Come on, you know. Things are going to be different."

"I suppose so," he allowed. "I'll have to handle the change like everything else in life that the Lord brings my way."

"Don't you think admitting the pain and discomfort would help?"

"I just did, and nothing changed. We still have to face things. Life goes on. We can either go with it or sit around feeling sorry for ourselves and discussing our hurts."

"You know that's misconstruing what I said."

"So what did you mean?"

"Doesn't the Lord allow us to mourn?"

"I did mourn when Dat passed."

For how long? she wanted to ask. *Two minutes?* "I'm saying we should be honest. Face the pain, and lean on others for comfort."

Marcus stopped eating and looked at her squarely.

"You think I'm not dealing properly with Dat's passing, and now Mam's marriage."

Mary met his gaze, unflinching. "Maybe I think there are better ways."

He wanted to push back, to tell her she was flat-out wrong, but instead he shrugged and jabbed his fork into a slightly undercooked potato. "I guess we are allowed our opinions."

She gave him a gentle smile. "Thank you for understanding."

He fell silent.

He obviously didn't understand. She tried again. "What are your plans when your mam weds? Are you staying on the farm?"

"We haven't decided yet."

"I guess this has come up rather quickly. No ideas?"

"There are," he said. "I could buy the place."

"You mean the farm you are living on now?"

"Yah. Why not?"

"Isn't that quite an undertaking for a young man?"

"Many of my friends have their own farms. Granted, they are wed, but I don't see why I can't manage it alone."

She forced a laugh. "I guess so."

"You don't think I can handle the load?"

"I think you're adding to the load. A bachelor's life? Why are you even considering that?"

"Apparently the Lord has those plans for me."

"Have you been in communion with him?"

"You are mocking me," he said. "I'm serious."

"I don't understand."

He fell silent again.

"I guess I don't have to understand," she added. "Sorry."

"It's okay," he said. "Things are what they are."

She leaned towards him. "That's exactly what I'm saying. They don't have to be that way."

He looked skeptically at her. "You do have strange ideas."

She ignored the barb. "Surely there is a prospect in the wings. You're not that . . ." She quit.

"Really?" He was looking at her. "Thanks for the compliment, at least."

"Well, it's true. You have . . ." She stopped again.

"What?"

"Potential. I mean . . . Look, this is not my place, really."

"Well, the Lord seems to disagree with your opinion on this matter," he said.

"Why?"

"There has to be someone available first, which there isn't. Not the right kind of woman, anyway." He looked away, his neck growing red.

"Is that so," she said skeptically, and then quickly drew back. "I'm sorry. I'm out of my place again."

He didn't answer for a long time, his plate empty. "You are thinking I am partly to blame?"

She kept her eyes on the floor, and didn't answer.

"Mostly, perhaps?"

She lifted her gaze. "Look. I have said too much already, like I usually do. My faults are many, of which this one is the greatest."

"Would you care to enlighten me on what you mean?"

Her heart was pounding wildly. Marcus had to hear the thumping in her ears.

"I am listening," he said.

"Are you changing your mind about me?" she deflected.

His smile was wry. "Let's say you are persuading me to consider another point of view. Are you not a teacher?"

"You don't mean that. Not really."

He reached over to touch her hand. "So why don't you tell me again what you think I should have done about Dat's passing, and now Mam's wedding?"

She couldn't move, let alone form coherent thoughts. "Perhaps we should talk a different time."

He looked around the room. "No one is paying attention. Now is fine."

She forced out a breath. "Well, for one, I could be a listening ear as you talk through your pain. I think this is what you need. Express your feelings and admit your suffering. That would soften you."

"And make me less critical?"

"I didn't say that."

"You didn't have to." He pulled away his hand.

She wanted to cover her head with her apron and scream. Had she blown the moment? "I'm sorry if I have said too much," she whispered.

"I'll have to think about this," he said.

Mary tried not to look at his face as Marcus stood. "There is dessert. Are you coming?"

Mary followed him back to the table, where a short line had formed in front of the pies and cakes, relieved to have a distraction. She had no idea whether the conversation had gone well or been a disaster. She only knew that she felt very odd.

Marcus stood waiting with Mary at his shoulder. The hum of the room filled his ears and his thoughts raced. Why had he opened up to Mary? Yet, he had meant every word that came out of his mouth, even if they had been strange ones. The woman had bewitched him, but on the other hand, maybe he was wrong? Maybe there were a lot of things wrong in his life, or as Mary preferred to say, things that could be improved upon. He didn't dare think further. The implications were too profound.

At least the woman was honest about her feelings. He had to grant her that, and deep down, he had to agree that Mary had a point. He could use softening. Life had been a heavy burden of duty he had carried about for many years. But then again, Mary didn't really know him, so why did she seem to think it was her job to "fix" him?

"These look like delicious pies." He managed a crooked smile in Mary's direction. "I've been looking forward to a piece of pecan pie since early this morning. Oh, but there's cherry too. I'm hungry enough for both!"

"Take a slice of each," Mary said.

"Really?"

"Yah, you worked hard this morning."

"Not more than usual."

"You earned two pieces. Give yourself some credit!"

"Is this the beginning of your lessons?"

"Maybe? I'm just saying."

"I think you're right." Marcus helped himself to the largest piece of pecan pie he could find, and then an equal portion of cherry pie, and Mary squeezed his arm gently.

Marcus didn't dare look at her. Nothing about Mary made sense right now—her lightheartedness, her kind eyes, her concern for him, her dazzling beauty, and now the touch of her hand. He wanted to stay close to her, and never leave, listening to the sound of her voice when she spoke. He would decide tomorrow if there was anything wrong with that. Right now he was a little overwhelmed, to say the least.

Mary followed Marcus across the crowded basement with their pie plates in hand and sat down on the bench beside him.

"Thanks for sitting with me today," he said.

She didn't dare look at him, lest this miracle disappear. Marcus was changing right in front of her eyes.

"Would you like it if I didn't light the fires in the morning?" he asked. "I could keep the wood bin filled from now on, and you could take care of things like you used to up north."

"You don't want to come into the schoolhouse anymore, every morning?"

"Not that," he said. "I like coming over, but I should have paid more attention to your way of doing things from the get go. I'm sorry. You're obviously quite capable."

"You think the school will be warm before the children arrive?"

"You get there early enough, I think." He made a face. "Sorry also about that misjudgment."

"You really mean this?"

"I do," he said.

"You would let me light the stove myself, and bank it at night."

"Don't rub it in," he said. "I'm trying to make right where I clearly was wrong."

"All this because I held your team back from breaking your wagon?"

"And much worse," he said. "And not just that. I misjudged you from the beginning, and I apologize."

"Wow." She let out her breath.

"You don't believe me?"

"I don't think you would fake words."

"Thank you," he said, without looking up. He finished his pecan pie. "I do need to change. You are right on that point, among many. Is it a deal with lighting the fires?"

"Yah, but one step at a time, okay?" Mary touched his arm lightly. "I should go help with the dishes. Shall I take your plate?"

"I need another piece of pie."

"You don't." She grabbed the edge playfully.

He hung on for a moment, his face lifted to hers. The depths of his eyes took her breath away. Mary clutched the dishes to her apron and rushed across the room.

Marcus watched Mary disappear into the group of women gathered at the basement sink. She made a point to stay out of sight, but that was okay. The day's events had caught both of them by surprise. He wasn't sure what had occurred. Talking about his feelings still seemed risky. He needed space to think things through, and obviously Mary felt the same. They were of one mind on that subject.

Marcus slipped out of the school basement, with one final glance towards the crowd of women gathered at the kitchen sink. Mary's form was not visible among them. He closed the door and stopped in front of the wood pile to collect his saw and coat. He stood there for a moment. The fresh stack of wood was a joy to behold, having sprung up like corn stalks in the summertime after a warm rain. They had cut more pieces than last year, since the farmers hadn't been able to work in the fields today, and almost everyone from the community had been here. He would have to remember that next year, and catch a Saturday after a rainy week. That wasn't always possible, but he could try. The least he could do was remember to plan the frolic, instead of forgetting like he had this year. That was so unlike him.

Marcus held his saw in one hand, with his coat draped over his shoulder, and headed out of the schoolyard back towards the woods, where his team was tied. The warmth of the afternoon sun crept into him, and a new thought crossed his mind. Maybe Mary was a stepping stone into the next phase of his life. Maybe she was simply a friend who was helping him to become a better person. That made sense, and was a much easier option to accept than if she were . . . He didn't even want to think the word—girlfriend, and eventually wife. That was a mountain impossible to climb, even with what had happened today. Mary was a teacher. That was easy to accept. She was preparing him to meet a decent community girl sometime in the future.

Seen from that angle, Mary had already been a great help. At least he was learning how to have a conversation with a pretty—no, beautiful—woman without getting all awkward. He shouldn't have tempted himself with the intimacies he had exchanged with Mary today. That went beyond friendship. He couldn't slip into considering their relationship something beyond friendship. Not today, and certainly not tomorrow. Marcus took care to keep his gaze away from the schoolhouse windows as he passed, forcing himself to whistle a nondescript tune. He stopped when he realized the merry sound coming out of his mouth was the jingle he associated with Mary.

CHAPTER 17

Mary awoke to the sound of rain lashing against the upstairs bedroom windows of the Hochstetlers' home. She pulled the covers higher under her chin for a moment. *Time to get up*, Mary ordered herself. A quick glance at the alarm confirmed that the loud, jangling racket would fill the room any second. Mary forced herself to push aside the covers and reach over to shut off the alarm. She got out of bed to light the kerosene lamp and stare blankly at the wall.

Leon had been right. "Looks like rain tomorrow," he had stated absentmindedly at the supper table last night.

From the sound of the wind this was a full-scale autumn storm. She had a heavy raincoat and hat prepared for the occasion, but regardless, the dash to the schoolhouse would not be pleasant. To make matters worse, when she arrived there would be no fire burning in the stove. That was her fault. Since the Saturday woodcutting, Marcus had kept his word. He no longer arrived at the schoolhouse before she did to light the fire in the stove. She had been allowed to assume her customary duties modeled after the years she had taught school in northern Ohio. In the excitement of the change, she had arrived earlier than usual to make sure the students noticed no difference in the comfort level of the schoolhouse. By the second week though, her euphoria had begun to wane. She missed Marcus's presence, which was a wasted emotion, since Marcus obviously had no intentions of having a relationship with her. Not that that was her plan, either. But maybe if she had shown him more affection the day of the woodcutting, they wouldn't have drifted apart? But Marcus hadn't been the only one overwhelmed with the feelings between them that day.

Mary sighed and changed out of her night clothes. She had to face things. Marcus was probably right in placing distance in their relationship. The idea that they both must have entertained that day, though briefly, that there could be more was—well, a farfetched idea. They were an impractical couple at best. If they were any kind of couple at all? Which they weren't.

She had survived quite well on her own those two years of school teaching at home. Things would soon be back to normal. She would get used to the silences of the schoolhouse in the morning, feeling the place undisturbed since she left the night before. The storm was upsetting her more than necessary at the moment. She had never thought to question the mornings at the old schoolhouse when she arrived to a building that was icy cold, from the night's dark hours without a fire in the stove. She had lit the kindling without hesitation, and soon had the flame burning brightly. She had stood in front of the stove with no thought of a man on her mind, rubbing her hands and feeling the heat from the wood fire creep through her body.

That had been before Marcus, of course, and his attentiveness, and his . . . Well, she would get over it. That was just that. She would have to. There was no other way.

Mary blew out the kerosene lamp and felt her way down the stairs. The soft glow of light from the kitchen soon lit her way.

"*Goot* morning," Lavina greeted her with a smile.

"It's raining," Mary replied.

Lavina laughed. "More like a washout. Even Leon wasn't expecting this, and he's the expert with weather forecasts."

Mary busied herself with the breakfast preparations.

"Do you want Leon to drive you to school?" Lavina asked.

"Of course not," she answered quickly. "I can walk."

"Just offering. Marcus might come by in his buggy."

"He won't," Mary replied without thinking.

Lavina gave her a sharp look and kept working.

Mary kept her face impassive, stifling the thrill that raced through her at the thought of Marcus pulling into the lane with his buggy. She would race out in the downpour and hop inside for the short whirl down the road to the schoolhouse.

"How are you two getting along?" Lavina sounded concerned, her head bent over the frying pan. "I don't see Marcus go up to the schoolhouse in the mornings anymore."

"That's because I asked him not to."

"Oh." Lavina was clearly disapproving.

Mary searched for words before offering. "I was used to taking care of things myself at my former teaching job."

"I see," Lavina said, although she clearly didn't.

Mary tried again. "I know that sounds, I don't know, independent, but we didn't have a janitor who showed up each morning back home. I thought I should get back to the way things were."

"Marcus wants to help," Lavina said. "He's good at that. You should let him."

"Did he light the fires for Susie?" Mary asked.

"I think so." Lavina appeared puzzled.

"Well, he has enough responsibility on his shoulders. The least I can do is lighten that load."

"I think the man cares about you," Lavina said. "You should let him show his affection in the only way he knows how."

"I thought you said Marcus did the same thing for Susie last year."

"He did, but the feeling is different with you. It means more to him."

An awkward silence gripped the kitchen, broken a moment later by the basement door bursting open and Leon plunging in from the outside.

"What is this, Indian monsoons?" he roared in mock anger.

"Breakfast is ready, dear," Lavina chirped back. "Get out of your wet clothes before you come into my kitchen."

"I'm wearing a full-length raincoat," Leon muttered, stomping down the stairs.

He was back in a moment, with his hair combed and in his stocking feet. "What a morning," he said, sliding into his chair and looking up at Mary. "Are you going to make it to the schoolhouse?"

"Of course! I'll be just fine."

"If Marcus were on the job, he'd come past," Lavina said.

Leon grinned. "That is a thought."

"Marcus should do no such thing," Mary retorted. "I am perfectly capable of walking up to the schoolhouse myself. You expect too much of the man."

"If you say so," Leon said. "Can we eat?"

Lavina looked very disapproving as they bowed their heads for the prayer of thanks. After the amen, nothing more was said about Marcus, or walking in the rain to the schoolhouse. Mary gathered her things together after the breakfast dishes were washed and brought her heavy raincoat up from the basement. Lavina helped her into the outfit.

"Be nice to Marcus if you see him," Lavina told her.

Mary nodded, and with her satchel under her arm plunged out into the storm.

Marcus paced the floor of the Yoders' barn. The morning chores were completed, and the storm still raged outside. Mose and he had made a mad dash into the house for a hasty breakfast and then returned to the barn, but there was little that could be done on a day like this. Mose was throwing down hay from the loft at the moment. There were still the horse stalls that should be mucked out, but the task could be completed by noon. The thought returned with urgency. He could easily drive Mary up to the schoolhouse. He knew her schedule well. She would be on the way soon.

Mary shouldn't be out alone in this storm, much as she loved her independence. He had chafed these past weeks, forcing himself to walk straight out to the barn after he awoke, instead of his customary trip up to the schoolhouse. This morning was too much though. Mary might already be at the schoolhouse, but he doubted if she was. The least he could do was walk with her, hold an umbrella over her head. He wanted to see her again. That was the truth. He couldn't help himself.

Marcus grabbed his heavy raincoat from the nail on the barn wall and slipped into the garment. He unhooked an old umbrella from the wall and rushed out into the storm. The wind had worsened since they made the dash to the house for breakfast, great squalls of water sweeping sideways through the air. He reached the main road and peered towards the Hochstetlers' place. There was no sign of Mary, but she could be hidden in the lash of the rain.

He headed towards the schoolhouse and had broken into a run when a faint form appeared in front of him. Mary. He overtook her a moment later. She was struggling with the wind, leaning sideways against the driving rain.

"Mary!" he hollered.

She whirled about, her face drenched, eyelashes dripping.

"Mary," he said again, and grabbed her arm with one hand and brought her under the shelter.

She didn't resist, and they ran side by side, stumbling towards the schoolhouse. Once inside, Mary huddled against the wall breathing hard while the rain ran down on the concrete floor from her wet raincoat.

"Thank you for that," she gasped.

"We should go into the basement," he said.

She nodded, leading the way.

"I'm sorry for scaring you out there," he said.

Her smile was crooked. "That's okay. I'm glad you came to help."

"I thought about the buggy," he said.

She waved her hand dismissively. "No, this is great."

"I'll light the fire."

"Yah." She slipped out of her raincoat. "I'll be up. Give me a moment to wipe my face dry in the bathroom."

He left his own raincoat in the foyer and had the fire burning brightly when her footsteps came up behind him.

He didn't look up. "I've missed this. You know that?"

"What? Lighting the fire?"

"Lighting the fire for you." He didn't face her. Was he saying too much? The words seemed to spill out with their own force.

"I can't say I didn't miss you," she said, "or rather, the knowledge that you had been here."

A strained silence followed. Marcus stirred the fire, with the heat rising to his face. The warmth justified the redness which he was sure darkened his features.

Mary shivered. "What a morning."

"The children will need help with their horses," he said.

"The storm might quit by then."

He laughed. "You're dreaming."

She nodded. "I suppose so. But don't you have chores?"

"Nothing pressing on a day like this. I'll wait," he said.

Mary couldn't believe she was standing in front of the warm stove with Marcus by her side. Marcus had the oven door open and the flickering flames danced before them in the cold schoolhouse. They stared into the fire in silence while the wind lashed the rain against the glass windowpanes. She wanted to reach out and touch him, to feel him draw her close again with the strength of his arms enveloping her this time. She wanted to say his name, and hear him whisper hers back.

A warmth that was more than the heat from the fire crept through Mary. She had to control these emotions. Marcus was just being nice this morning. It was nothing more.

She clasped her hands to keep them from reaching out on their own. "I'm glad you showed up though."

From the look on his face, Marcus appeared under the same spell from their bewitching circumstance, so she was not losing her mind.

"Maybe we can both help the children unhitch," she suggested.

He glanced over at her. "That would be great."

She kept her voice to a whisper. "You can light the fire again each morning, if you wish. I would like that."

"You sure?" He was staring at her.

"Yah. Unless you don't want to."

"I would love to come up each morning. It's really no trouble. Maybe I could even . . ." He paused, gathering his courage. "Maybe spend a few minutes with you."

Mary didn't look at him. What did that mean? She forced a laugh.

"I won't make a nuisance of myself," he said. "I didn't mean it that way."

"You're not a nuisance. I like having you around."

He shifted on his feet. "I try to make myself useful wherever I am."

She opened and closed her mouth several times. His closeness with the fire burning in front of them was becoming too much. "I should look at my lesson plan for the day."

He nodded. "I'll light the lantern. It'll still be dreary when the children get here."

They worked, ignoring each other, or at least trying to. Marcus went into the basement once he had the lantern humming on its ceiling hook. He puttered about down there, probably keeping himself busy, and away from her. She had been too bold, and Marcus had said too much. They both had been caught in the magic of this rainy morning. Magic went away, and life continued. This would all look so different tomorrow once the sun came out again.

Mary focused on her lesson plan until the first student drove into the driveway. The black buggy appeared like a ghost out of the mist, the horse shaking his head in protest from the lash of the wind on his face.

Marcus had Mary's raincoat ready when she came down the steps. She was making an effort to look out the window, anywhere but where he stood.

"You don't have to help me," he said. "It's still bad outside."

"I want to." She finally met his gaze.

He gave in with a bob of his hat. He wanted her by his side. He desperately did. He had resisted the urge for the last thirty minutes down in the basement to rush upstairs and tell her how *wunderbah* he thought she was, and how beautiful. He forced himself to move and open the door. Too many things had already been said this morning by the warm stove, with the fire flickering in front of their eyes. He must not embarrass himself further.

"Let's go," he said, and they dashed across the yard together.

CHAPTER 18

THE BALL GAME ON THE SCHOOLHOUSE FIELD WAS IN FULL SWING THE following week. Mary shielded her eyes with the flat of her hand, standing behind home plate, concentrating on the incoming pitch. Marcus's sister Esther had become quite the expert pitcher since the beginning of the term. The third-grader had the characteristics of her older brother—his determination, his steady hand, and his focus on the task at hand.

Lamar, one of the eighth-grader, was up to bat, but Esther wasn't flinching. The ball sailed in the air and came slowly in for the hit. Lamar swung, but failed to make a solid impact. The result was a grounder towards first base instead of the home run fly ball Lamar must have envisioned. Esther didn't hide her glee while the first baseman ran out, caught the grounder, and almost beat Lamar back to first.

"That was a nice pitch," Mary hollered to the happy girl.

Esther did a little jig on the pitcher's mound, stopping only to catch the ball thrown back to her.

Lamar roared his displeasure. "I'll get it right next time!"

Mary shouted her encouragement. "Don't let him scare you!"

Esther prepared herself for the next pitch. Out of the corner of her eye, she caught the sight of two figures heading their way from the Yoders' farm. She turned for a better look, and the pitch faltered.

Mary stilled the sharp intake of her breath. Marcus and his brother Mose were headed across the field. What could the two want? They didn't appear in a hurry or alarmed. She hadn't seen much of Marcus since that rainy morning last week, when the combination of storm and fire had so mesmerized them. Marcus must have known the passing nature of their emotion. She certainly did. He was back to lighting the fire in the stove each morning, but he hadn't gone out of his way to stay until she arrived at the schoolhouse, and she certainly wasn't going to show up early just to catch him. Her feelings about him were getting to be quite confusing, but she knew she didn't want to appear overly eager. No sense setting herself up for embarrassment and disappointment.

"Maybe they are coming to help us play," a student suggested.

Mary cringed. She had been trying to forget what happened that rainy morning, and the things they had said. To make it worse, she had almost reached for the man's hand again. What if Marcus knew how much she would have welcomed his embrace?

"He is quite the ball player," the student declared.

Mary brought herself back to the present. "Keep going," she hollered to Esther.

The girl shook her head. "They've come to play with us. I want to wait."

No one else on the field was moving either. They stood with eager faces turned towards the two approaching Yoder men. This was a sunny Friday workday for the farmers. Marcus would never walk away from his duties. Maybe he wanted one of the eighth-graders to help on the place for a few minutes?

Esther began squealing and waving her arms around as Marcus and Mose slipped through the fence. "Hurry! We're waiting!" she ordered her brothers.

Both men obliged and broke into a slow trot.

"I'm picking Mose," Esther hollered. "He's playing shortstop."

The two halted, and Marcus sent a warm smile her way. "Is it okay if we play, teacher?"

"Sure. Why not?" Mary tried to hide her confusion. "You're here, so join in. But . . ."

"Give me a glove," Mose hollered, trotting across the field. He expertly caught the glove someone tossed him. Marcus approached home plate with a sly grin on his face.

"You're really going to play?" Mary's head was still spinning. "I haven't seen you all week."

Marcus appeared not to notice the irrelevant comment. "I couldn't resist watching such fun going on right under our noses without joining in."

"You're done with your farm work?"

Marcus wrinkled his brow. "Let's say we're caught up for the moment." Marcus waved his hand for Esther to throw the pitch. "Let's go."

Esther concentrated and the ball sailed across home plate.

Charles, one of the first-graders, swung and managed a solid enough hit towards shortstop. Mose scooped up the ball and easily made an out on first.

"Number three," someone shouted, and the sides began to switch on the field.

"Where am I supposed to play?" Marcus asked.

"Shortstop." The answer came without hesitation.

"Looks like it's tit for tat," Mary told him. "Unless you can't play?"

He grinned and didn't answer, trotting over to take his position. Mary went towards first, which was the position she'd been playing this week. Marcus noticed and waved. "Can you catch?"

She stuck her nose in the air and didn't answer, but her heart was pounding in her chest with Marcus's teasing. She desperately wanted to impress him the way she had at volleyball. Why did she care so much what he thought of her?

Mary held her place, waiting for the game to begin. Marcus would be throwing a ball her way. That was inevitable. She couldn't fumble. Much seemed to hang on her success. But what could happen? Marcus wouldn't criticize her. She could even imagine him being perfectly understanding if she missed a thrown ball that landed right in her glove. Had last week changed their relationship that much? Or the week before? The touch of his hand, or hers in his? Such little things, those moments by the fire. Had they been transformed?

The whack of the ball pulled Mary out of her thoughts. The hit was a high fly ball over second base, and the outfielder was never going to make the catch for an out. A throw to first was the best anyone could expect. Mary concentrated, the beat of the runner's feet in her ears. She leaned forward with her foot on base for the ball that came hurtling towards her. The solid thump in her glove came a second before the rattle of the runner crossing the plate.

"Out!" several voices shouted.

Mary threw the ball to the pitcher. She had made the play, and Marcus was smiling. She felt a rush of joy and satisfaction so strong she was nearly giddy

Marcus grinned, watching Mary's excellent play at first base. She didn't surprise him anymore with her abilities. He had learned to expect the best from her, although Mary probably didn't know that yet. She had taken his teasing well a moment ago. He hardly ever teased, let alone Mary. Why couldn't things have been like this when he first met her at the bus station? Mary was not to blame for their conflict. He was. He should never have made such a big deal of the stupid suitcases.

This was a big step today, coming over to play ball on the schoolyard. He hadn't dared make any overtures since those sweet moments spent around the stove that rainy morning last week, where the wonder of her presence had overpowered him and stirred feelings he didn't know existed. Too many questions buzzed unanswered through his head. Was he falling in love with Mary? That didn't seem possible. He had been mesmerized by her, which was just infatuation, and that was dangerous territory. But she certainly didn't seem dangerous today, playing ball and laughing with the kids. Goodness, this was all so confusing. Soon the noon-hour ball game would be over and he would return to the safety of his world until the weekend, before he would see Mary again.

"Coming your way," someone shouted, and Marcus focused on the game.

The grounder arrived fast, and he bent low to scoop up the ball. With a twist on his heels, he came around and sent the ball towards first base. Mary was ready, her face intent, and she didn't fumble.

"Out." The holler was clear.

Two plays later they made another out together when he threw the ball to Mary on first base. They made a team, apparently. Mary was laughing and smiling, obviously thrilled with her plays.

"You catch well," he told her on the way to home plate.

"And you throw well," she said, sending the compliment back.

Marcus pulled his watch out of the side pocket. "We have ten minutes left."

"You hoping to bat?" she teased.

"Yah," he admitted. "I kind of was."

"Then you will," she informed him, turning to say, "Marcus will bat third. Let's get two runners on base."

Marcus planted a smile on his face and banished the turmoil of his thoughts.

"Thanks for coming over." She returned his smile. "Should we be expecting you here more often?"

"We don't often have a chance," he said. "But I would love to."

"You're welcome anytime."

She turned her attention to the first batter, who managed to make first base. The second sent a fly ball between first and second, near enough to avoid the lunge of the outfielder and far enough to stay out of reach of the first baseman. There were now two runners on base.

"Your turn." Mary handed him the bat. "Let's see if you can get them home."

"Nothing like a little pressure," he said.

"You can handle it."

Marcus gripped the bat. He usually enjoyed playing ball, but Mary made him feel something more: alive, strong, like he could pick up a thousand hay bales on a hot summer day and never break a sweat. Her eyes made him dizzy with their blue sincerity. He had to stop thinking about Mary, or this would never work. The first pitch he let go by, and prepared himself. The second ball was too low, and he passed again.

"Come on now," someone hollered, but he blocked out the sound.

The third pitch was to his liking and he swung with the full power of his work-hardened muscles. The ball connected in a solid whack and sailed skyward to hang suspended against the sun. He stopped following the track and raced towards first. The ball was still in the air when he rounded the base, so he kept going. The players were searching the back field at second, and he crossed home plate before they found the ball in the bushes.

"That wasn't even fair," Mary scolded, but her eyes glistened with admiration.

"You asked for it." He winked at her, and couldn't believe his boldness.

Mary blushed bright red, and whirled about to give the order. "Someone run and ring the bell." She took a moment, turned away from him. Her face was still flushed when she faced him. "Thanks for coming. That was fun."

"We'll have to do it again."

"There is the farm work," she demurred. "I understand that."

Before he could answer she was moving away, ushering her students in front of her. Marcus stood rooted at home plate until Mary disappeared inside the schoolhouse door. He wanted her to turn and wave, to give him some acknowledgment, some something. He knew that things between them could never go beyond friendship, but he wished they could. For the first time he wished with his whole heart, but there were things no man could change. Certainly not Marcus Yoder. Mam would marry in a few weeks, and he was no closer to finding a wife than he had been at the beginning of the year. With a heavy heart he followed Mose back across the fields to his farm duties.

CHAPTER 19

THE ALARM CLOCK JANGLED LOUDLY ON THE MORNING OF THE WED-
ding. Mary leaped out of bed to push back the bedroom drapes.
School had been dismissed for the day, and the first streaks of
dawn were on the horizon. The sky was clear above the rising sun. Across the fields, the windows of the Yoders' build-
ings were bright with lantern light that flooded into the yard.
The dim outline of buggies being unhitched could be seen. The
cooks were arriving, no doubt, and other relatives who wished
to help with the last-minute details. Marcus's mam would be
wed today. Before noon, Silvia Yoder would be, for the second
time, a married woman.

This would be a solemn and serious day of commitments.
Silvia would walk into the future with another person by her
side, a man who would be there until the Lord called one of
them home. Mary had not crossed that border into the land of
marriage even once, yet alone twice. Did the journey become
easier the second time, fraught with less danger, perhaps? The
choice of a marriage partner should be easier than her experience indicated. Others seemed to find the journey almost pain-
less, while she had turned away many suitors, waiting for the
perfect one. Maybe that was her problem? Maybe there was
no perfection? Yet her heart had begun to view Marcus with
great admiration. He appeared almost perfect to her, which she

knew couldn't be true, which led her to doubt all of her feelings and instincts. Was he really the arrogant, critical man she had encountered that day at the train station, or was he the thoughtful, hardworking, sweet man she had come to know since? How could she trust her own feelings when they had changed so dramatically in such a short time? The confusion was torture. She was thinking about him way too much. Most every day in fact, stealing glances towards the Yoders' place during the school children's play hours.

Marcus and his brother Mose hadn't been back to join in the games. Not that she expected them to. Grown men didn't have time to leave their farm work during the day for foolish activities, and there was the extra work the wedding had imposed on the Yoder family. Still, she had wanted Marcus to come back. He was slipping in and out of the schoolhouse in the early morning hours before she arrived. What had happened to the hint of spending a few seconds with her? Was she supposed to change her routine and arrive earlier? That seemed risky and fraught with even more danger. There were so many questions and so few answers. They had both been touched with the magic of that rainy morning in front of the fire, but life was more than magic. Marriage was meant to be practical, and Marcus and she were not practical together. She knew that. So did Marcus, which was why he stayed away from her. That was the logic of the situation, which her heart didn't accept, obviously. Neither did the community. Both thought that they were a perfect match. She had only to think about Marcus standing by her side that morning near the stove, only inches away, so close and yet so far, to feel her heart rate increasing with a longing she couldn't put words to. They had almost crossed an invisible barrier that morning. Just beyond lay an embrace in each other's arms. There would be no turning back then.

Mary pinched herself and stepped away from the window. Better sense had prevailed, but she was still tormented by the question. What would have happened if she had reached for Marcus's hand that morning? What would being wrapped up in Marcus's arms feel like? That was a question best unanswered, which was why she had come to her senses. They were not meant for each other. Her heart was wrong. There was simply no other answer. The road to marriage should not be this complicated, which confirmed a thousand times their unsuitability. Wasn't Silvia Yoder demonstrating that truth today with perfect clarity? Around noon, Silvia would reach for the hand of John Beachy with a smile on her face and promise to honor and love the man, right there before Bishop Mullet and everyone else. She could never do that with Marcus. There would never be enough magic moments in front of open stove doors on rainy mornings to carry them through life together.

Mary wiped away a tear to dress and hurry down the stairs. She had promised to help Lavina with the breakfast preparations this morning, since everyone wanted to arrive early for the wedding.

"*Goot* morning." Lavina looked up with a smile when Mary burst into the kitchen.

"I was . . ." Mary caught her breath. "I was looking out the window. The buggies are gathering already."

"The cooks, yah." Lavina's eyes twinkled. "How are you doing?"

"Okay. I'm fine. Why?"

Lavina shook her head. "Did you know that Marcus bought the farm, now that his mam will wed?"

"He mentioned he might." Mary busied herself with getting the eggs out of the refrigerator.

"I expect he'll set up house for the time being by himself," Lavina continued. "But the man can't do that for long. A male alone in a house isn't decent, not with the cooking, baking, and washing. He can't stay a bachelor for long, I'm thinking."

Mary didn't answer. What was there to say?

"At least Marcus asked you to have a part in the wedding today. Be one of the special table waiting couples."

Mary took a quick gulp of air. "Silvia asked me. It's her wedding, and it seemed the logical choice, with me being the new schoolteacher."

"That's the same thing," Lavina said.

"Ah, I don't think so."

"Wedding days are such sweet moments." Lavina ignored the objection. "Your day will come soon, dear. Marcus is more than willing, even with his gruff ways. Take that from a woman who knows the man quite well."

Mary's mouth moved, but no sound came out.

"*Goot* morning," Leon bellowed up the basement stairwell, and Mary jumped.

"*Goot* morning," Lavina hollered back. "The wedding bells are ringing across the fields."

"That they are," Leon agreed, and came up the steps to give Mary a bright smile.

She looked away as her face burned with a rush of heat. Leon had overheard their conversation. She was certain. When she snuck a glance at him a moment later, he was grinning like a cat that had gotten into the butter.

Across the fields, Marcus met another buggy pulling into the Yoders' driveway. The first rays of the sun had burst above the horizon, flooding the yard with a promise of brilliant sunlight to come.

"Good morning," he greeted the elderly cook.

"I'm running a little late," Wauneta grumbled. "Don't tell me I'm the last of the cooks here."

"I wasn't counting." Marcus dodged the loaded question.

She looked around. "Well, I'm not the first one, that's for certain, and on Silvia's wedding day. I'm glad your mam has finally made up her mind."

"Mam's happy with her choice," Marcus responded with a smile.

Wauneta wrapped her shawl around her shoulders and bustled up the sidewalk. The woman had lived alone in her children's *dawdy haus** since her husband's passing a few years ago. He couldn't remember exactly when. Those were things blocked out of his memory. They reminded him too much of his own loss. At least Monroe Miller had lived a long life, and seen his children to full maturity.

Marcus ignored the pain that throbbed inside of him. He undid the tugs and led the horse forward to push the buggy into line. He shouldn't think about Dat this morning, on the day that Mam planned to take another husband. He had enough problems accepting the change. John Beachy could never be his real dat. That place was already taken. Maybe Mam had waited until now to wed so he wouldn't have as much of an adjustment? This way, he would never have to live in the same house with a new man sitting in Dat's place at the head of the table. Planned or unplanned, Mam had given him that much. Maybe the Lord's grace had guided Mam without her knowledge? That seemed possible. Still, he worried about his younger siblings. This was a lot for them to adjust to, too.

Marcus moved towards the barn, leading the horse, lost in his thoughts. This place would be his next week. The rest of the family would move, after Mam had spent the week alone at John Beachy's home. There were no honeymoons in the Amish world, but newlywed couples usually had the privacy of their homes without children present. Since this was not the case, Mam would be given a little time with her new husband before the two families were united.

---

* Part of a home or a separate house designated for elderly parents to live in on the adult children's property.

Things would not be easy from there, but Mam and John would manage. They fit well together. He had to admit that, even with the ache of Dat's parting still in his heart. Mary was right on that point. The hurt was there, and he was paying attention now. If that helped, he wasn't sure. Perhaps Mary was stirring up more trouble than she was doing good? He still wondered in moments like this.

Marcus pushed open the barn door and stepped into the flood of lantern light.

Mose appeared, coming back from taking another horse to the stalls. "Is that the last cook?"

"I don't know. Wauneta seemed to think so."

Mose grinned. "That woman is always the last one to arrive. She'll be late for her own funeral."

Marcus managed a chuckle.

"I'm going in for breakfast," Mose informed him. "Before the real rush starts."

"I'll be right after you."

He took Wauneta's horse back to the stalls and tied him to the wooden railing. The barn would swell with horses in an hour or so. They would have to take the overflow out into the barnyard and down the side fences.

Men from the community would take over this task after breakfast. Both of them had duties for the day, which required their presence in the house well before the service began. They were part of the kitchen detail, which would help the cooks move the food out to the serving area this morning and wait on the tables after the ceremony.

Marcus checked the tie rope before he moved away from Wauneta's horse. The last thing he needed on this busy day was a loose horse in the stalls tormenting the others and causing a general ruckus right in the middle of the preaching time. Things would be done decently and in order on Mam's wedding day, even if he was hurting.

Marcus left the barn and shielded his eyes against the brightest of the sun's rays. There was not a cloud in the sky, a sign no doubt of the Lord's good favor. But on the other hand, many couples had wed on rainy days and had experienced long and blessed lives together. He would be with Mary today. He had been trying not to think about how they would relate for those long hours together. Would there be embarrassment? Mam had asked Mary to serve as a table waiter, and he had been the logical choice as her partner. The memory of Mary's sweetness, standing beside him that rainy morning near the schoolhouse stove, still lingered, and he couldn't understand that. The flickering flames had been to blame, he had told himself a thousand times to no avail. He would not object if life consisted of smooth sailing, but he knew better. Dat's death had driven home that point. Tragedy was usually just around the corner.

Mary was an aberration, a vanishing vision, and he didn't want that. He had never wanted unreal living. He couldn't give in to temptation now, not after the time he had spent waiting for the Lord to bring a proper woman into his life. If he gave in, his temperance would go to waste. Mary wanted, deep in her heart, some other kind of man. What kind, he didn't know, but Mary would be unhappy with him once the flickering flames died down, as they always did. Mary would be miserable, in fact. He was certain.

Marcus entered the house to find the usual bustle on a wedding day. Women were flittering about everywhere, with dough-covered aprons and rolled-up sleeves.

"Breakfast is in the basement," Wauneta hollered at him, waving her arms about.

Marcus gave her a warm smile. The woman might have arrived last, but she immediately made herself the center of activity. He peeked into the kitchen.

"Can't go down that way," Wauneta informed him. "Use the outside basement steps."

Marcus retreated, pausing on the front porch. A figure hurried across the fields toward him. He stared, longing stirring in his heart. Mary was too far away to notice his attraction. He would be working around her the whole day, so he had to lasso his emotions into submission.

Marcus tore his gaze away from the approaching figure, shimmering in the glow of the rising sun's rays, and rushed down the basement steps.

CHAPTER 20

As the church service continued, Mary sat beside Marcus on the hard backless bench. Bishop Mullet was about to conclude his sermon, if the clock on the wall was a proper guide. Only fifteen minutes remained until twelve o'clock. With so much scheduled after the marriage vows were spoken, weddings weren't supposed to drag past the noon hour, even if the bishop in charge waxed eloquent with his sermon.

Mary snuck a quick glance at Marcus. His face was impassive, as it had been for the entire morning. She was certain he had fled into the basement as she approached the house early that morning. If she had known he would be grumpy, she would not have agreed to serve as a table waiter today. Not when the duty entailed the whole day spent at Marcus's side. They might not be a couple, but couldn't they at least be friendly toward each other?

Mary forced herself to listen to Bishop Mullet. "Man and woman were created by the hand of God Himself," the bishop was saying in his measured manner. "The Almighty fashioned out of clay the figure of the man, and blew the breath of life into him. When Adam lived, the Lord declared it would not be *goot* that he should be alone. A search was made for a companion among the beasts of the field, but none was found. So the Lord God placed Adam into a deep sleep, and out of his side took a rib, and from the rib the Lord God made woman, who would be a helpmeet, a hand to hold his, a mind to think with him, and a support in the darkest hours of his life. Marriage is a holy and sacred institution, for it comes from the mind of God Himself. We are called to keep our marriages pure and undefiled before the eyes of the Lord. That is our most urgent call, and I believe our brother and sister seated before us today have taken this weighty burden into account when they have agreed to walk the rest of the days the Lord God may give them, together."

Bishop Mullet paused to catch his breath and focus on John and Silvia, seated in front of him. Mary snuck another glance at Marcus. His face was tense, and his hands were clasped tightly. The man was suffering. She had forgotten about that aspect of this day. Marcus's mam was replacing his dat. Of course he was tense. She should comfort him, not criticize. Did she dare? What would Marcus do if she reached for his hand? They had touched before. Marcus should not object, and he'd understand what she meant by the gesture.

While Mary hesitated, John and Silvia stood in front of Bishop Mullet to say their vows. Marcus's eyes were fixed on the hardwood floor, his face like stone. She was correct in her conclusions. The man was burying his feelings deeper than the bottom of the sea. Mary moved her hand slowly. He flinched when she slipped her fingers into his hand, but didn't make a sound. She leaned closer, until their shoulders touched. She moved her fingers across his calluses, finding the rough spots scattered among the tenderness of his palm. She caressed them with her fingertips. He didn't move. She dared glance up at him quickly. There were tears on his cheek. Marcus was crying?

His fingers finally responded to hers. He traced the outline of her hand, cautiously at first, as if he trod on dangerous ground. Somehow Mary understood. She was a world he knew nothing about, even feared, a part of his heart that had been frozen and locked away for years. More tears appeared on his cheeks, dripping onto their hands. He held hers as if he never planned to let go.

John and Silvia finished their vows and took their seats again. A song number was given out, and the first note filled the air. Mary's fingers stayed in his as the music drifted through the room. When the last note died, Marcus pulled his hand away. Mary gave him a warm smile, and mouthed, "How are you doing?"

He didn't respond, as the service concluded and the line of table waiters stood to exit. She stayed by his side. He wasn't angry. She was sure of that. Marcus was hurt by the circumstances of life, and she was here to comfort him. That made a lot of sense. She wouldn't allow herself to think beyond this moment.

Marcus was conscious of little else but Mary's presence on the walk across the yard to the barn loft where the meal would be served. Several of the couples in front of them were laughing and exchanging pleasantries after the completion of the three-hour church service. Any words stuck in his mouth, even as the memory of Mary's hand in his, back there on the church bench, burned in his mind. The circles of warmth from her fingers had reached deep into his heart, into places he didn't know existed. His chest throbbed with the pain and the joy at the same time, in some strange swirl of emotion that left him dizzy.

"Thanks for being here today," he said into the space between them. He didn't dare glance at Mary.

"It's okay," she said. "I'm sorry for what you are going through."

He wanted to reach for her hand again, but he didn't dare. "Mam is married," he said instead.

"I know it's not easy for you," she whispered.

How did Mary know? The tears stung, as they had during the service.

"Thank you for your kindness," he said as the line swept into the barn loft. The couple in front of them leaned towards each other for a moment, their eyes shining with happiness, but they were dating. He did not have that sort of relationship with Mary.

"It will get easier," she said, walking close to his side. There was more she wanted to say, but this time she held back. He didn't need a lecture right now.

He gulped, and followed the others as they entered the curtained-off section of the barn loft. The cooks were busy, intent on their tasks, with kettles and pots sitting everywhere. Marcus paused along the wall, and Mary did likewise. He could feel her presence so near, and yet so far.

"There will be plenty of food, looks like," she whispered.

He released the air from his lungs. "Yah, there will be."

Wauneta appeared and waved her arms about. "Table waiters eat quickly," she ordered. "Back here. There isn't much time."

Marcus let Mary lead the way this time. It seemed right, somehow.

They seated themselves, and a quick prayer of thanks was offered. The food was placed on the table in front of them. Mary pulled the bowls close and offered them to him. He filled her plate first.

Her smile was coy. "Not too much."

"You need to eat," he answered.

He took his time, allowing the magic of the moment to fill him: her hands holding the bowls, her face so close and so open, the chatter of the room around him.

"You doing okay?" she asked.

He managed a smile. "Yah, I'm okay."

"You sure?" They began to eat.

"I feel better now."

She looked very skeptical.

He couldn't tell her why. *Your touch is healing.* That seemed quite inappropriate. How were such words spoken to a girl? To Mary, in particular?

"I guess I'm relieved that I don't have to move over to the house with the rest of my siblings," he managed instead. "But I'm kind of worried about them, too. They're used to having me around, you know?"

"You won't be far away."

"It feels like I'm avoiding something." He gulped down his food. "Like I'm running away."

"Perhaps you've been responsible for them long enough. Your mam wants you to live your own life, to have your own family."

"That is in the hand of the Lord," he said.

"We can still take steps in the right direction. Like buying the farm and living there. That's a start!"

"That is its own form of pain."

"Maybe? But better."

He nodded. "You have a different way of looking at things."

"I'm right," she said with a knowing smile.

"I'll have my hands full with the farm."

"You'll do just fine."

"Are you just saying that to make me feel better?"

"No. I believe in you."

"You shouldn't say that."

"I will say what I want to say."

He laughed. He liked that about her, her confidence.

"Come." Mary reached for his hand. "The others are leaving and we have to help."

He tripped on the bench on the way up, and disentangled his fingers from hers. She was beaming up at him, and he let her lead the way again.

Mary paused at the curtain into the dining area with Marcus close by her side. She nearly hugged herself with excitement.

Their relationship was moving forward, and Marcus was not objecting. She was breaking through his defenses to someplace beyond.

She had seen his heart today, and what she saw was tender, kind, caring.

"Let us give thanks for this noon meal," Bishop Mullet announced from the tables set up on the other side of the curtain.

Everyone bowed their heads, and Mary reached for Marcus's hand during the brief prayer. He didn't let go until the amen was pronounced. He also didn't look at her, but that was okay. They lined up at the serving table to get their plates of food.

"Potatoes and chicken plates are right here!" Wauneta was directing traffic.

Mary filled her hands, and Marcus did likewise. She stilled her emotions before their venture into the other side of the curtain. She must not show too much joy. Marcus had not agreed to anything. The man might hold her hand, but that was still far, far away from a formal date.

"Ready," Marcus stated more than asked.

"Ready," she said, and they marched out together, plates in hand, with bright smiles on their faces.

Marcus was smiling on his mam's wedding day. She had gained a greater victory than she had dared imagine possible.

Marcus tried not to trip on his own feet as they swept across the barn loft to their assigned table.

"Anybody want food?" Mary sang out in the sweetest voice he had ever heard.

The magic was back, the light and lofty feeling he had experienced beside the flickering flames that rainy morning. Mam's wedding day had brought them back, the day he had first held a girl's hand in something more than friendship. He wasn't in love yet. That wasn't possible. He was swept up in the magic of a wedding day. How else could he explain this feeling?

Marcus set his plate on the table. "There you are. I have the potatoes and Mary has the chicken."

The woman in front of him appeared not to hear a word. She was beaming up at them. "What an honor. This table is being served by the loveliest couple in the whole community. Both of you practically glow with happiness."

Marcus smiled and nodded. He didn't dare glance at Mary, as cold waves washed over him. Was Mary objecting? The community had long viewed them as a couple, but there was something official about the words today. He whirled about without checking and made a beeline back to the curtain, with Mary behind him, obviously struggling to keep up.

He feared a sharp rebuke from her lips once they were safely out of sight. He took his place in the line and squared his shoulders to wait.

"Your mam has a most lovely wedding day," she said.

He dared sneak a glance at her.

"There is hardly a cloud in the sky," she said with the brightest smile. "I peeked out when we dropped off the potatoes and chicken."

"It is a nice day," he said, and forced himself to breathe evenly. Mary was not objecting, and he was seeing her for the first time as his girlfriend. Someone he could love. The world would never be the same.

CHAPTER 21

THE SATURDAY MORNING A WEEK AND A HALF AFTER THE WEDDING, Mary slipped out of the house the minute the breakfast dishes were washed and put away. Lavina gave her a teasing smile. "I'll be up with Leon in an hour."

Mary felt the heat burning on her neck, and once she was outside, turned her face into the gentle breeze drifting up from the south. There was no shame in the feelings she had for Marcus, and even the weather agreed, wrapping its warmth around her. It was unseasonably warm for late November and there hadn't been a drop of rain since Silvia's wedding, as if the Lord wished to bestow His abundant favor on that union and on marriage in general. She had not always agreed with such sentiment, but something had shifted within her since Silvia's wedding. What a blessed display of the Lord's grace Silvia's marriage had been. The Lord was indeed restoring and healing hearts. Silvia's happy face last Sunday when she greeted her children at the church service had made everyone in the room smile. Today the two families would be officially united, after Silvia's belongings and her children were moved over to John Beachy's place. John's children would be returning from a cousin's home, where they had been staying since the wedding.

Mary slowed her steps. Marcus had been waving to her this past week when she walked back and forth from the schoolhouse, but beyond that had not made an appearance. The weather was to blame, she had told herself, at least partly. The smallest fire in the stove took the chill out of the air in the mornings. Besides that, the fall field work was in full swing, which was always a rushed time for the farmers before winter set in. Marcus and Mose had been out with their teams from the crack of dawn until the time arrived for the evening chores. She had seen Marcus go back out to work in the fields after supper. She should have gone over and offered her help with the chores, but she hadn't dared. She had done what could be done on the day of the wedding. Marcus must be given time to absorb the realities of their new relationship. She was at peace. The Lord was in charge, and there was no rush. Marcus had come a long way since she set foot in the community, and, she had to admit, so had she. She could wait.

The memory of Marcus's touch in her hand lingered. She had savored fully his closeness, his smile, and his strength. She had so wanted Marcus to broach the question of their future on the day of the wedding, but he hadn't. Marcus had to feel what she had felt, and would open his heart fully to what work the Lord was so clearly doing in both of their hearts. She would have to show him that the way was safe. That despite their obvious differences, there was hope.

"How are you doing?" Mam had written this week.

"Okay," she had written back. Mam wanted to know more, but the time to write about Marcus and the feelings stirring in her heart had not arrived. She could hear the questions her sisters asked Mam when they met at the monthly sewing or the Sunday services.

"Is there any sign that Mary has found love?"

"Has she mentioned meeting someone?" another one doubtlessly asked.

"It has to happen," Esther would say in her all-knowing voice.

Heat crept into Mary's face thinking about Marcus. She slowed her walk even more at the Yoders' driveway. Marcus was handsome, and a good catch. He had a deep voice and an honest heart. Her sisters would be impressed. There was no doubt there. She could already hear Lois coo, "I see that waiting was worth it for you. That's what you've been up to?"

Mary quickened her steps when a buggy appeared in the distance, followed by another one. In front of her, the barn door opened and Mose appeared.

"You're early," he said with a tired grin.

"Not really." She motioned over her shoulder towards the arriving buggies. "So are you ready for the big move?"

Mose shrugged. "This is the only home I've ever known, but it's okay."

"Life moves on." Mary tried for a lighthearted tone.

"It does," he agreed. "Marcus will have the full load of the farm on his shoulders."

"You might come back to help sometimes?" She tilted her head at him.

He nodded. "I told Marcus I would, at least for this fall. A few weeks, you know. He hasn't agreed. Not yet."

"He can be stubborn."

Mose laughed, and moved toward the arriving buggies. "Marcus is in the barn finishing the chores," he said over his shoulder.

It was an invitation of sorts, even if Marcus had not said the words. Mary opened the barn door and moved into the dusty interior, following the thumping sound of stalls being mucked out. Marcus was bent over his fork when she turned the corner, but appeared not to have heard her approach.

"*Goot* morning," she said when he paused to catch his breath.

He turned with a tentative smile. "How are you?"

"It's a beautiful morning for your mam's move."

"That it is." He straightened his back.

"How are you doing?" she asked. "Hard at work, I see, as usual."

He laughed. "What else is there to do?"

"Ah . . ." Mary hesitated. She wanted to say, *Living. Enjoying life. Loving people.*

"You are early," he said.

"Leon and Lavina are coming soon. Looks like there will be plenty of help."

He nodded. "The community at its best."

"The Lord's blessing is on your mam's marriage. You know that, don't you?"

He smiled. "I am thankful for how that day turned out. You were there and . . ." He seemed to falter. "It wasn't as hard as I expected."

She stepped closer. "The Lord is a great healer. He is showing mercy right now."

"The Lord is," he agreed. "Especially with me taking on the full duties of the farm."

"I am here to help," she said with her gaze on his face.

"And I am thankful for that, very thankful."

Relief filled her.

"I should finish here," he said. "The buggies are arriving."

"What can I do?"

"There is another fork over there," he said.

"That way you'll finish sooner."

"But you don't have to help."

"I want to."

He gave her a quick glance.

"I do," she said.

"But why?"

She held her breath. The moment seemed precarious, as if their gains could be washed away in a breath. They were discussing more than physical labor.

"I want to," she said simply.

He pondered the answer for a moment. "Seems like there should be deeper reasons."

"Is that why you are hesitating?"

"I have my questions," he said. He seemed to understand her perfectly.

"Is the Lord's will a sufficient answer?"

"You think the Lord cares about us, enough to bring us together, to this place, to . . ." He faltered again.

"The Lord cares about you."

"About us?"

"Why should He not?"

"We're not important."

"The Lord decides why He does what He does. Don't you think?"

"Maybe?"

"He does," she assured him.

Marcus seemed to acquiesce. He bent his back to the work, and she joined in. The thump of muck being thrown into the wheelbarrow filled the stall as they worked in silence.

"Help us, dear Lord." Mary sent the prayer silently heavenward. "Help us open our hearts to each other."

Marcus threw the last forkful of muck from the stall into the wheelbarrow and straightened his back. He gave Mary a quick smile. "Thanks. That was helpful."

Further words stuck in his mouth.

"Whoa there," Mose's voice hollered from the barn door as he brought in the arriving horses.

"I should go help." Marcus motioned towards the front. "You want to come with me?"

"Of course." Mary didn't hesitate.

They met Mose coming in. "How are you two doing?"

"We're all done," Mary chirped.

Mose grinned. "You two make a *goot* team."

Marcus hurried on as Mary lingered behind him, holding the stall door open for Mose.

"You look lovely this morning," he could hear Mose saying.

Those were words he should be saying, but the very thought left his mouth dry. "Thank you." He could see Mary gazing up at Mose with a bright smile on her face.

Marcus forced himself to wait at the barn door until Mary appeared.

"Your brother is so charming," Mary gushed. "I'm surprised some girl hasn't snatched him up yet."

"Mose is kind of young to date," Marcus muttered.

Mary laughed, and he soaked up the sound. At least she wasn't suggesting that she should be the girl who returned Mose's charm. He was jealous of his brother. That was the truth. But he loved him, too.

Marcus pushed open the barn door and headed across the barnyard with Mary close beside him.

"*Goot* morning," Marcus greeted the next arriving buggy.

Bishop Mullet and his wife, Pricilla, were inside, smiling their brightest, as if they approved of the whole world, and in particular the appearance of this young couple in front of them to help unhitch their buggy.

"Looks like we have curbside service this morning," Bishop Mullet declared, and hopped down the step, still spry for his age. The bishop hurried around the buggy and offered Pricilla a hand.

Marcus fumbled with unfastening the tug, but Mary was smiling at him when he glanced up, as if his clumsiness were the most charming thing in the world.

"I'll take things from here." Bishop Mullet positioned himself at the horse's bridle. Marcus was left holding the shafts, with Mary still smiling at him. He let go to a rattle of wood on the driveway. Shafts should be let down slowly, not released like a five-year-old without the strength to hold on.

"Next." Mary motioned towards another buggy entering the driveway, appearing once again not to notice his mistake.

Marcus followed her, with Mose soon joining them at their labors. The yard was full of buggies thirty minutes later. Several hay wagons arrived with prancing teams, eager to head back down the road with their cargo once things were loaded. The wagons were backed up to the house and the furniture appeared. The men wrapped the items in blankets to position them on the flat beds.

"They really are moving," Mary mused as they caught their breath, standing alone and watching the activity. "It won't be the same around here tomorrow morning."

"I know," Marcus said.

"You'll be okay. I know how capable you are."

"That's nice of you to say." He let out his breath.

"It is true, you know. Your capabilities."

"We should talk about that," he said, suddenly very serious.

"Your capabilities?" Mary looked at him quizzically.

"About my struggles with our relationship, my incapability to deal with what is clearly happening between us." The words tumbled out quickly, as if he'd been holding them in too long and could no longer bear the burden of them.

Mary paused, considered her words. After a moment she replied soberly, "There is no rush. The Lord will lead us."

He forced a smile. "Life goes on."

"You don't have to keep saying that. I understand. I really do. You have a lot of changes to adjust to right now. It might not be the right time to . . . to start a friendship." The words caught in her throat. She meant them, but she also desperately hoped he'd tell her she was wrong, that it was the perfect time.

"Why are you being so nice to me?"

She pulled herself together, determined to change the mood to a more lighthearted one before she dissolved into tears. "Because I'm a nice person."

He looked at her. She was teasing. They both laughed.

"You don't think me crazy then?"

"Not at all."

"You expect things to really change then?"

"They already have, haven't they?"

"I guess so, but I feel foolish talking about my problems so much."

"You don't have to. The Lord gave us friends to share the load."

"I know I have things to sort through, but we are becoming more than friends. You know that, right?"

"Do you object?" She tilted her head at him.

"No."

They looked at each other for a long moment, allowing their eyes to lock, to speak everything their words couldn't at that moment. Until finally Marcus broke the spell, laughing a little.

"But you and me? Who would have thought?"

"The Lord and His mysterious ways."

"Is that always your answer?"

"Maybe? It does fit."

He nodded, agreeing. "We should go help with the loading."

"I'll go work in the house," she said, but it was another moment before she willed herself to walk away.

He followed her progress to the front door before he approached the wagon to grip the side with both hands and cat-apult himself upward. What had just happened between them? Had he committed himself to Mary? This was the girl of the shimmering suitcase. A cold sweat broke out on his arms.

"About time we get some help," one of the men scolded. "Lovebirds have to come down from the clouds someday."

Marcus forced himself to laugh and grabbed the edge of the couch the men were carrying.

CHAPTER 22

Later that day, Marcus's mam and her belongings had been permanently moved to John Beachy's home. In the falling dusk, Mary lingered in the yard, waving to Lavina and Leon as they walked out of the driveway. Mary hadn't seen Marcus since the noon meal had been served in the yard, where the community women had made full use of the waning Indian summer day's warmth. Marcus had kept his distance while Mary helped serve the sandwiches and chocolate milk prepared for the gathered movers. Laughter and happy chatter had drifted across the yard and upward towards the open heavens. Mary had joined in where she could, but her laughter quickly died away whenever her thoughts turned to Marcus. She must exercise patience, to match her bold words this morning. Marcus was still at a crossroads, in spite of her intense desire that he move on. She should be at his side this moment, or close at least, but she must give him the room he needed. The Lord would have to finish the work that had been so clearly begun. In the meantime, she must bear the wait as Marcus worked through his fears at his own pace.

Lavina, who must have noticed her predicament, whispered in her ear, once the movers had left, "You should stay and serve supper for Mose and Marcus. I heard Mose say he'd help with the milking and then spend the night. I'm not sure he's too eager to move into the new place, to be honest."

"Serve them supper?"

"Marcus shouldn't object," Lavina had encouraged her. "Someone left a casserole and a pecan pie. The casserole just needs to be heated up, I expect."

Mary swallowed the lump in her throat and waved one last time at the retreating Hochstetlers. Leon had left with a smile on his face, so he must fully approve of Lavina's suggestion that she stay to fix supper for Marcus and Mose.

Mary sighed and turned towards the barn. She pushed open the door, and the hinges squawked loudly, as usual. Mose looked up from herding the cows into the barn.

"Ah, help has arrived," he said, grinning.

"I thought I'd stay. You must be tired from moving today."

"Not more than usual," he said. "But I am glad you stayed behind."

"And there is supper, of course. Casserole. Which you could heat yourself, I suppose."

"We don't know how to turn on the oven," he said, and they both laughed. "I'll have the feed down in a moment." He turned to go. "Marcus will be around soon."

Mary picked up a three-legged stool and stood along the wall, waiting, as the soft lowing of the hungry cows filled the enclosed barn space. Marcus wanted her to stay. Deep down he did. She would have to believe that until proven otherwise.

Marcus paused behind the horse stall with a bale of hay clasped in both hands. The weight hung heavy on his shoulders, but he barely noticed. Mary was standing against the far barn wall, obviously waiting for the milking to begin. She had stayed after everyone else had left. Warm circles raced around his heart, the first pleasant emotion he had felt since the fear that had gripped him after their conversation this morning. Marcus shifted the hay bale as the strings cut into his ungloved palms. The agony of the day had been severe. Life without Mary had become like the desert landscape he had seen in pictures back during his school days. There the weather was hot and the sand dry, without an oasis or green trees in sight. That's what his life had been like before Mary arrived in the community. He hadn't known back then, but he knew now. He didn't want that existence anymore.

Marcus kept looking at Mary standing against the barn wall, waiting for Mose to feed the cows, and the pain in his heart seemed to fade into the distance. The beauty of Mary's spirit washed over him, and her soothing presence touched him again, deep in his heart. He must move forward in his relationship with her. There was no other choice. Seeing Mary like this, he knew. She was here tonight, and he felt like getting down on his knees right here on the barn floor in thanksgiving for the Lord's grace. During the lunch hour he should have offered her a smile while she served the sandwiches. That was the least he could have done. He could not assume that she would continue to extend her hand of friendship forever.

Marcus repositioned the bale of hay and stepped around the corner. Mary's gaze flew up.

"You stayed," he said, trying to sound lighthearted.

"I did."

"I'm glad."

"Oh." She was smiling now.

"I'm sorry about today." He forced the words out and set the bale of hay on the barn floor.

"We got your mam moved," she said.

"I appreciate everything about our conversation this morning. I should have told you at lunch time."

Both of them jumped when Mose hollered, "I'm back!"

Marcus turned to face him.

"Everything okay?" Mose asked with a concerned look. He set down the wheelbarrow of feed.

"Everything's fine," Marcus told him. "Mary is helping with the chores."

"And supper," she said.

Marcus was certain there were tears on Mary's cheek.

Mary managed to give Mose a smile. He appeared ready to say something more, but he must have changed his mind and began to shovel feed to the cows. Mary didn't look at Marcus as she chose the closest cow and sat down behind its haunches.

"I really am sorry for the way I acted today," Marcus came up to say quietly.

Mary took several deep breaths, before she peeked out from behind the cow. "I forgot a milk bucket."

Marcus's startled look almost made her laugh. The day had been long and difficult for both of them.

"I'll get one." He hurried away. "I want to change my ways," he told her when he came back. "For your sake, for both of us, for what is right."

"It's okay. We'll talk about things later."

He didn't say anything more, retreating from sight. Mary placed the bucket under the cow's udder and began to draw down the milk.

"Are you okay?" Mose asked at her shoulder.

"Yep," she chirped.

"Okay," he said, appearing completely unconvinced.

Mary ducked behind the cow again, and Mose moved on. Her face was flushed with happiness. Marcus had apologized for his behavior today, and his words had been laden with total sincerity. He had turned a corner in their relationship, or crested the mountaintop. Either way, something had changed. Mary peeked around the cow's haunches. Marcus's broad back was in view, busy milking his cow. His shirt was barely soiled from the day's work of carrying heavy furniture out of the house and onto the wagons. Not too many men would be so clean tonight. Marcus had worked hard. She hadn't ridden with the teams over to John Beachy's home, but Marcus had made several trips on the back of the wagons to guard against any accidents on the rough side roads. There was a weariness written in the slump of his shoulders, but little more. Marcus was a special man. There was no question there, and he was willing to change when change was the right choice.

Mary turned back to her milking and stood when the bucket was full to the brim with the foam threatening to spill over the top. She walked carefully over to the strainer perched on top of the milk bucket and emptied the contents without losing a drop to the floor. She could feel Marcus's gaze fixed on her. Everything felt brighter, like the sun had broken through the clouds. She was dizzy with the feeling, and nearly lost her grip on the bucket.

Mary collected herself and spoke in Marcus's direction. "I'm going inside to get supper ready."

"I'll see you in a little bit," he said.

She couldn't resist looking at him. "Unless you want me to help with another cow before I go?"

His smile was gentle. "We're fine, and don't feel that you have to serve us supper. We can fend for ourselves."

"I disagree with that," Mose hollered from two cows down.

Marcus laughed. "I guess you had better stay."

Mary set her milk bucket on the floor. "See you shortly, then."

She hurried out of the barn door without looking back, her heart overflowing with joy.

The stars had come out by the time they sat down to eat supper that evening. Marcus sat at the head of the table where Dat used to sit. Mam had occupied the place since Dat's death, but she was gone now. As if Mary read his thoughts, she gave him a sweet smile.

He swallowed hard and looked away. "Let's pray and give thanks."

They bowed their heads in silent prayer.

"Amen," Marcus pronounced a few moments later.

They lifted their heads, and Mary shyly passed him the casserole.

"Hey, don't I get to eat?" Mose protested. "I did work today."

"All in its *goot* time," Mary said, her voice soothing.

Marcus lost himself in the soft tones, barely managing to keep his grip on the edge of the casserole bowl. It was the effect of the day, he told himself, and his tiredness, and . . . well, Mary. He might as well be honest.

"There is something special coming after the casserole," Mary said.

"I don't see anything special." Mose dished out a generous helping of casserole.

"That's because the pecan pie is in a covered dish."

"Pecan pie!" Mose's face lit up.

"I take it you're a fan?" she asked.

"My favorite," Mose mumbled, his mouth full. "Or at least right up there close to the top."

"And you?" Mary turned towards Marcus.

He tried to keep his thoughts straight, but all he could see was Mary's tender smile. "I . . . Pie is . . . I like a lot of them."

"He gets tongue-tied around beautiful girls," Mose said.

"And you don't?" Mary shot back.

Marcus smiled at the startled look on Mose's face, and then took pity on the rising color in his cheeks and shifted the conversation.

"Mose is a *goot* brother," he said. "He has stood shoulder to shoulder with me during these difficult years without Dat. Tonight is our last night together, with the memory of Dat heavy in our house. Tomorrow we part ways, and I suppose things will never be quite the same."

"I thought you said he gets tongue-tied," Mary said in Mose's direction.

Mose shrugged, smiling a little. "I'm ready for the pecan pie!"

Mary passed the pie to Mose first, and he grinned, helping himself to a very large piece.

"I think you took two pieces," Mary chided.

"There's plenty left for you and Mose," he replied, looking very unrepentant.

"I guess this is a special night," she relented. "What about you, Marcus?"

He met her gaze. "The usual, please."

She cut the piece and transferred it to his plate.

"This is so unfair," Mose complained. "I had to cut my own."

Marcus forgot about his brother and even the pie in his mouth as Mary took her own piece and they ate. He could not take his eyes off of her face. Mose seemed to sense the solemnness of the moment and remained silent.

When they had finished with the last crumb, they bowed their heads for another prayer of thanks.

"I'm helping with the dishes," Marcus said after they lifted their heads.

Mose grinned and vanished upstairs.

Mary gave him another smile and stood to her feet. "I wash and you dry?"

"Sounds *goot* to me," he said. "And I'll help clear the table."

"Do you know how?" There was teasing in her voice.

"I can avoid dropping the plates," he shot back.

"I'm sure you can." Her back was turned to him, standing at the sink, running the hot water. The cool evening breeze blowing through the screen played with the loose strands of hair hanging down her neck.

Marcus picked up several plates and carried them to the counter.

"You didn't drop them." Her sly smile turned his throat dry.

He moved back to the table and gathered up the utensils. She joined him with a washcloth, moving her hand across the vinyl table top. He watched transfixed.

She caught his gaze. "Is the table clean enough?"

He wanted to take her in his arms, but he didn't. "Everything you do is beautiful."

Mary ducked her head and finished the cleaning.

He went back to the counter and found a drying cloth.

She was at the sink when he returned. "It's been a beautiful day," she said.

"Yah, it has," he agreed.

"The weather couldn't have been better."

"Will you be going home for the Christmas holidays?" he said, changing the subject.

"Maybe. Mam did ask in her last letter, but I haven't decided. Should I?"

"Everyone goes home for Christmas."

"Will you be home with your mam?"

He thought for a moment. "I guess that is a proper question. Things have changed."

"Same predicament I'm in," she said. "My first time away from home for the holidays."

"You strike me as a world traveler."

"With my glowing luggage." Her laugh was strangled.

"No, with your mature attitude. You strike me as a person who has seen the world."

"In books," she said. "Not much else."

"I would like to, sometime," he said. "Maybe take the Greyhound bus on one of those thirty-day tickets that go anywhere in the US. One of my uncles did that in his younger days."

"You're still young," she said.

He wanted to slip his arm around her waist and pull her close, but he wiped the dishes instead.

"I should be going," she finally said, the last dish stacked in the cupboards. "The morning will come soon enough."

He walked her to the door. "Shall I take you home in the buggy?"

She laughed. "That's funny. I haven't worked that hard."

He dared touch her fingers on the doorknob. "Good night," he whispered.

She moved down the porch steps, calling over her shoulder. "I'll see you tomorrow in church."

He stayed at the door a long time, trying to catch a glimpse of Mary's form hurrying across the fields in the starlight. He was certain he saw her several times, but perhaps he was imagining things? Perhaps he had imagined everything today? The whole world appeared a haze in the fallen darkness.

CHAPTER 23

M ARY SLIPPED INTO THE SCHOOLHOUSE ON MONDAY MORNING, HER breath fogging the glass pane of the door. The weather had turned colder over the weekend, as if to make up for the unusually warm past few weeks. She closed the door and cleaned a spot on the glass with her elbow. She peered out across the playground. Fast-moving clouds scurried across the sky. Snow would be moving in later in the day, if not sooner. Silvia had chosen her wedding and moving dates well. Today, the furniture on the wagons would have been transported under tarps. Even that might not have been enough to keep things dry if the snow blew hard enough. Clearly the Lord had blessed Silvia down to the smallest details.

Mary turned to pull off her coat and froze at the sound of footsteps on the upper schoolhouse level. She let out her breath slowly. Those were Marcus's footsteps. He must have decided to light the stove on this stormy morning and stayed to speak with her. Marcus was still serious about moving forward with their relationship. Mary's heart pounded at the thought. She was in full agreement. Silvia was not the only one in the community who had been given a miracle from the Lord's hand.

The footsteps on the upper floor came closer. "*Goot* morning." Marcus's deep voice filled the entryway. "Hope I haven't startled you."

Mary made a face at him. "I thought it might be you."

"Mose came over last night," he said. "Looks like he might be helping me part-time. He might even move back for part of each week. Turns out there isn't enough work to keep him busy at John's place. Or maybe he just misses me." Marcus gave a playful smile.

"That's wonderful," Mary gushed. "I am so glad for you."

He turned more serious. "I guess I do need help, and I'll pay fair wages."

"You are always fair, and needing help carries no shame."

"I suppose not." He managed to smile. "I had a few moments free, and decided to come up.

"I'm so glad. We didn't get a chance to speak yesterday."

"I know," he said. "It was *goot* to see you at the services, though."

"Now you're here."

He laughed, and sat down on the top step. "How are things going?"

"Okay. What about you?"

"There's not much that can happen in a bachelor's life," he said. "At least interesting things. Just the farm work as usual."

"The house must seem empty."

"It does. But I'll get used to it."

"I should stop by and make supper for you and Mose again tonight."

His face brightened. "You would?"

"If you want me to?"

"There is no question there. I mean, if you have the time. But you were just there on Saturday evening."

"There's nothing wrong with my coming over tonight." She seated herself beside him. "I would love to stop in."

"There's still casserole left from the moving day," he said.

She glared at him. "I'm making something proper, believe me."

"Don't trouble yourself—we'll just be happy with the company."

"No Amish man turns down *goot* cooking."

"That is true," he agreed.

"I may not be able to match your mam." She tilted her head at him.

"You can cook," he said. "You're an Amish woman."

"And if you're wrong?"

"I'm not wrong."

"Confident, are we?"

"Confident in you."

She slapped his arm. "That's a changed tune."

He took her hand in his. "I'd be honored to have you cook for us. But my real happiness will come from you just being there. The house is empty and forlorn by myself, and even with Mose there. It feels like it's lost its best occupants, which it has."

She couldn't break her gaze from his eyes. "It's only been a couple nights. You'll get used to it, I'm sure."

"I don't know," he said. "Mose and I sat eating by ourselves last night at the kitchen table. I mean, the food that the community had left for us was *goot*, and we managed to heat it in the oven without burning down the house, but nothing else was right. Mam and the kids were gone, with their laughter, their chatter, the sound of their footsteps. Men weren't made to live alone."

"I can't come every evening and make supper for you."

"I didn't mean to imply . . ."

"How about twice a week. I can handle that."

"You would?"

"With great joy in my heart. My schoolwork has slacked off since I have more of a routine and have gotten used to the children's ways."

He stood to his feet. "Then I should be going with such a concession in hand, but you do know that I didn't come to beg for help."

"I know that." She gazed up at him.

"Can't wait then," he said. "Just come when you can."

"It'll be four or so, I'm thinking. From there, let's keep the evenings in question a surprise."

"I like that," he said, "and if some weeks you don't have the time, that's okay."

"At least I'm coming tonight." She followed him to the door.

He paused with his hand on the doorknob. "Thank you for coming to our community, for teaching school here, for . . ."

She waited. She could almost see the thoughts swirling behind his eyes, then changing direction.

"I'm sorry again about that first day when I picked you up at the bus station. I said things I shouldn't have."

"It's okay. That's behind us now."

"I guess it is."

"It is," she assured him. "We have grown since I arrived. You have changed, but so have I."

"You have changed?" He appeared very skeptical.

"I did. I had ideas which were wrong."

"You want to talk about them?" He had a twinkle in his eye.

"So you're saying what's *goot* for the gander is *goot* for the goose?"

He laughed. "Something like that. But we can talk later. When you're ready, or maybe not at all. Whatever suits you."

"Thanks for your consideration, but this is the truth. I arrived determined not to look for a relationship with a man. I have changed my mind. You changed my mind, of all people. Who would have thought?"

"I know," he said. "Life seems to get stranger by the day."

"Are you objecting?"

"No. I am glad, but it feels like things are changing so fast, my head is spinning."

She laid her hand on his arm. "We have all the time in the world. I'll be over tonight in time to make supper, and perhaps even help with the chores."

"Supper is enough," he said. "Especially after a full day of teaching. Stop in at the barn before you go up to the house, will you?"

"Of course."

Marcus tipped his hat and closed the door. Mary waited for his backward glance and waved through the glass. He appeared dazed, but happy. Mary hugged herself.

She wanted to take him home for the Christmas holidays. The urge swept over her. Mam should meet Marcus, and her sisters should lay their eyes on the man. Heat rushed into Mary's face. Their teasing would be unbearable.

"Slowly, Mary," she whispered. "Slowly, slowly . . ."

Marcus peeked out of the barn window soon after three o'clock to see the schoolyard full of departing buggies, and Mary's form among them, obviously helping the children leave. She would be over soon, if he didn't miss his guess. Supper made from scratch wasn't a small affair. He knew that much about cooking. He should feel guilty for imposing on Mary's time, but the anticipation of seeing her again so soon overpowered any other feelings.

"What are you doing?" Mose's voice teased from behind him.

Marcus didn't say anything. The answer was obvious. Mose laughed and moved on.

"Mary's coming over tonight to make supper," Marcus hollered after him.

Mose gave a thumbs-up over his shoulder. "Way to go. When are you two officially dating?"

Marcus avoided the question yet again. He didn't know. His fears still haunted him at certain moments when he was alone, so the best way forward was to take his time. Mary seemed agreeable to that tactic. So why should anyone else object?

An hour later Mary stuffed the papers she had to check into her bag. They could wait until later. She would have an hour or so free to work after she arrived home after supper at the Yoders' house. She wanted plenty of time to prepare, because this supper must be the best meal she had ever made. Marcus claimed he didn't need to see how well she could cook, but they were still young in their relationship. She wanted to impress him. She imagined him filling his plate a second time, telling her everything was just perfect. He would be thinking ahead to all the meals they would enjoy together as a married couple.

Mary hurried out of the schoolhouse and up the road, scolding her own thoughts for moving too quickly. Yes, their relationship was progressing, but they were not even officially dating yet, and there had been no talk of marriage.

There was no sign of anyone working when she passed the Yoders' fields. It would only take a few moments to reach the Hochstetlers' and change out of her school dress. She burst through the front door, startling Lavina, who was working in the kitchen.

"Is something wrong, dear?"

Mary caught her breath. "Not at all! I'm going to make supper for the Yoder brothers tonight."

"How did that come about?" Lavina asked, clearly pleased.

Mary skipped the question. "I have to make my best impression. I'm thinking mashed potatoes and gravy, a roast, fresh rolls, corn . . . oh, and chocolate cake, or do you think apple dumplings would be better? Maybe with molasses cookies? Perhaps I should call a driver to get me to the store more quickly. Oh dear, I may need to just buy a dessert at this point. I don't want dinner to be late."

Lavina had never seen Mary so scattered. She smiled to herself, but spoke with the kind of authority that comes from years of experience. "However this happened, you need to calm down. You're making too much of a fuss. A simple casserole is *goot* enough."

Mary shook her head. "They still have leftover casserole from moving day. I want to do something special."

Lavina thought for a moment. "I suppose you're right, but not a roast and mashed potatoes on a Monday afternoon. There is too much risk, I'm thinking."

"What then?"

"Something simple. How about what I'm making for our supper, baked chicken and scalloped potatoes? Shoofly pie for dessert? The boys will find that nourishing and delicious at the same time."

Mary hesitated, clearly not convinced.

"You're only missing the chicken. I saw what Silvia left the men last week in their pantry. Here, take some chicken from me so you don't have to go to the store. Then you'll have time to make the pie."

Mary saw the wisdom in her suggestion, smiling at the thought of baking for Marcus. She imagined the smells wafting through the kitchen as the boys came in from the chores. She knew she could make a mean shoofly pie with a buttery, flaky crust and a rich, gooey molasses filling. It wasn't fancy, but it would hit the spot. "I can't thank you enough. I really can't."

"Anything to help along your budding relationship," Lavina said with a smile. "I was beginning to lose hope in Marcus."

"We're moving slowly, and rushing in headlong at the same time."

Lavina chuckled. "Those are the best ones, sometimes. Go change and get over there."

Mary rushed upstairs and was back in ten minutes. Lavina had the chicken ready in a paper bag and had added a Tupperware container of biscuits she'd baked earlier in the day. Mary gave her a quick kiss on the cheek and plunged out the door. She hurried across the field and, arriving at the Yoders' house, pushed open the squeaking door and hollered inside, "I'm here!"

Marcus appeared at once, his face and shirt covered in straw. A grin spread across his face. "Sorry for the way I'm looking, but I'm glad you came."

"I suppose supper goes down well either way," Mary teased. "At least my supper does."

He didn't laugh. "We'll clean up before we come into the house."

She shook her finger at him. "Nothing more than you would if your mam was making supper."

He hesitated. "Okay. What is for supper?"

"Secret," she chirped, and closed the barn door on him before Marcus could ask any more questions.

An hour later, Marcus waited impatiently as the last cow made her cumbersome way out of the barn. He brushed another piece of straw from his shirt.

"You're spotless," Mose commented dryly.

Marcus didn't answer. Working in the barn didn't leave a man exactly clean, but they were both hungry.

"Let's go eat," he said.

Mose was already on the way, and slammed the back barn door shut. The cows lowed softly behind in the barnyard. They walked together across the darkened yard, towards the house where a light burned brightly in the kitchen window.

"Are you finally dating the girl?" Mose asked.

"She's making supper for us."

"You'd better not let her get away from you," Mose warned.

"I'm not planning to," Marcus told him, surprised at the vehemence in his own voice.

"That sounds better." Mose held open the door of the wash room, and they entered. A small kerosene lamp was burning at the sink.

Mose grinned. "What service do we have tonight?"

"What do you expect?" Marcus shot back.

Mose's grin grew. "The man is changing his tune. I like this."

"Just wash," Marcus retorted, and waited his turn.

The table was set as usual when they stepped into the kitchen, with the supper dishes spread out on the vinyl tablecloth.

"Surprise," Mary chirped.

"Chicken and scalloped potatoes!" Marcus seemed genuinely pleased, taking his seat at the head of the table. "And is that shoofly pie I smell coming from the oven? How did you have time to make all this?"

Mary smiled, arranging the warmed rolls on a plate and taking her spot opposite Marcus.

"There is nothing better than chicken and potatoes," Mose added.

Mary couldn't contain the warmth she felt spreading through her. Everything had turned out just right. The chicken thighs had crispy, golden skin, and at the last minute she'd found a jar of green beans in the cupboard, which she heated on the stove, then sprinkled them with salt, transferred them to a serving dish, and placed a large dollop of butter on top to begin melting. She had arranged the sliced potatoes neatly in concentric circles in a pie plate and then smothered them in rich cream and fresh eggs that she had whisked together. Then she'd added grated cheddar cheese, which now bubbled invitingly on top.

Marcus forced himself not to stare at Mary, turning his eyes down as they bowed their heads in silent prayer. A great joy filled his heart, and words of thankfulness wanted to burst out of his mouth.

He sufficed with an "Amen," but wanted to add a thousand more. He gave Mary a warm smile instead.

She glowed with happiness, passing the food bowls to him first. He helped himself, slowly, lest he spill on the table and embarrass himself. When he finished, Mary took the bowls from his hands and passed them to Mose. Only then did she fill her own plate. Marcus ate, and couldn't believe how much he had come to love and admire this woman.

CHAPTER 24

MARY LINGERED ON ELMER MILLER'S FRONT PORCH SWING AFTER the hymn singing that first week in December. Light from the gas lanterns inside streamed through the front window and across the floor in a soft glow. The happy chatter of the young people was a distant whisper through the house walls. A few of the steady couples had their horses hitched to the buggies, and the girls were getting ready to climb in and leave. She had watched this scene often back in the home community, but never with this longing in her heart, or with a full understanding of what created the intense interest between the dating couples.

Her sisters would chuckle if they could see her now, sitting here alone, wishing that Marcus would come out of the house and join her. Of course, once they set eyes on Marcus they would understand fully. She was sure about that.

"A perfect fit," Esther would say.

"Couldn't have found someone better for you myself," Phoebe would add.

Lois would nod and agree.

Mary Wagler had found a man she wanted to date. The problem was, Marcus was taking his time. She wanted him to drive her home in his buggy on an official date tonight. Desperately! She had dropped what hints she could. She had cooked supper for the men twice a week for a while now. Those were moments of great joy, and Marcus was charming or attentive at his house, but she was getting impatient. Perhaps she should not have told him that there was no rush.

This past Friday evening, she had held her breath at the kitchen sink while he wiped the dishes beside her, thinking the moment had arrived when Marcus would ask. He had come close. The words had been in his mouth, she was certain. But they never came out.

"I enjoyed the evening a lot," he had told her at the door in parting. "Thank you so much for doing this each week. I can't say how much it means to me."

Marcus meant every word of thanks. She didn't doubt him. Now, as other couples swooned all around her, she was keenly aware of her longing to make the relationship official. She began to push the swing with her feet. The squeak of the chains in the still night air was loud, but no one inside the house would hear her, occupied as they were with their conversations. Most of the dating couples had begun to leave in their buggies. If anyone came out on the porch, they would hardly notice her seated in the shadows. She could watch Marcus leave, driving away with Mose in his buggy. She could sit here the whole night in sorrow and sadness and never go home to sleep.

"Here you are."

Mary jumped. She hadn't heard the front door open.

"Marcus!"

"Yah," he said. "I wondered where you had gone."

"I'm just sitting here enjoying the evening."

"It's a nice evening," he said.

"I should be going though."

"You want me to hitch up your horse?" He tilted his head towards the barn.

Sit down beside me on the swing, she almost said. Men could be so obtuse.

"Shall I?" he asked, still waiting.

"Maybe later," she said.

He looked around. "It's not too chilly for December."

"It's been an odd season—warm one day, cold the next."

"There is snow coming again, before Christmas I think."

"Are you the weather forecaster?"

He laughed. "No, just a farmer, and using the *Farmer's Almanac*, which could be wrong, of course. Snow for Christmas would be nice though. I have the outside farm work caught up."

"Snow for Christmas is always nice."

"It is," he agreed, still standing. "Have you decided about going home for the holidays?"

"Not yet." Mary moved her hand from the empty space on the swing, careful not to glance down. She was not going to drop another hint. He was going to have to take some initiative sooner or later.

Marcus shifted on his feet. He wasn't sure what he should do. He didn't want to break the precious few moments he was spending with Mary on Elmer Miller's front porch, but more young people would be coming out of the house in a moment. Not that he was ashamed of anyone catching him talking to Mary. Most everyone in the community already considered them a couple. They just weren't officially dating.

"You should stay here in the community for Christmas," he said, bringing his thoughts back to the conversation.

"Why?"

She appeared more beautiful in the shadows of the lantern light than he had seen her in a long time. Of course, he was becoming more enamored with the woman each passing week. He no longer had moments when he would vow to never think of Mary as anything more than a friend.

"Can I sit beside you?" The thought took shape in his mouth.

"Maybe? If you answer my question."

"Well . . . Mam could have us over for a big breakfast. Sort of celebrate her new beginning and all."

"That would be nice."

"There are also other options." He motioned towards the front window. "I'm sure Lucille will have a big doings here for their family. Lucille will extend an invitation the moment she learns you are staying."

"You may sit." Mary's hand patted the empty space beside her.

Marcus sat down and the chains squawked above him. He held his breath. He didn't dare look at Mary. The front door opened and slammed shut. Several young men hurried down the steps and headed towards the barn without noticing them.

"The moon will be up soon," Mary said once they were gone.

He followed her gaze. There was a soft glow on the horizon that bubbled up like a balloon. "I guess it will be," he said. "I hadn't noticed."

The front door slammed again, and two girls emerged, giggling as they walked towards the buggies being hitched in front of the barn. They would be discovered soon, and he wanted this conversation to continue. Even more, he wanted to linger in Mary's presence.

"Let me take you home tonight," he said, his gaze still on the horizon.

"I have my buggy to drive."

"I guess you do. What am I thinking?" His mind whirled.

"You could follow me home in your buggy," she said.

"That would be a little strange."

"Maybe so," Mary said, feeling more frustrated than her voice revealed.

She continued pushing the swing with her feet.

"On second thought, who cares if it's strange?" Marcus said, a new energy in his voice. "Let me follow you home, and perhaps stay for a bit."

"Of course," Mary said, too quickly, as if afraid he'd change his mind again. And then she appeared to hesitate. "But I didn't make anything for us to eat."

He glanced at her. "So what?"

"You need something to eat on a date."

"I had supper," he said.

"But there should be something special. On our first date. I could have baked brownies or cookies, if I'd known . . ." Her voice trailed off.

He stifled the urge to apologize. "You are special enough," he said.

She wasn't looking at him. "Do you really mean that?"

"I wouldn't say it otherwise."

"I know."

"Then is it a yah? Taking you home, and coming into the house."

She smiled, a ghost of a smile, as if she was surprised and shocked that this was happening.

"I'll get your horse then." He stood to his feet. She followed him down the porch steps. He reached for her hand, and she clutched his fingers. He left her at the hitching post, waiting. "I'll be right back."

So this was it? He had never imagined how he would date a girl like this. The idea that had taken root in his mind had been about something proper and well planned weeks in advance. Certainly not a date entered into on a whim, the decision made sitting on a front porch swing with the moon rising on the horizon. Yet, that was exactly the kind of life Mary had introduced him to: different, fascinating, a little impulsive, and excruciatingly sweet at the same time.

Mary studied the rising moon on the horizon while Marcus was in the barn. She wasn't imagining this moment. Marcus was taking her home. Yah, in his own way. This was much more original than anything she had ever heard her sisters say about their first dates. Those sounded like formal affairs, with the request made weeks in advance, which always produced a flurry of baking in the Waglers' house and a thorough cleaning far above the usual Saturday sweeping and dusting. She had experienced none of that, but what she was experiencing couldn't be any less exciting or romantic than her sisters' first dates. She had never heard them talk about a moon rising, timed perfectly to herald the arrival of fresh hopes and dreams. She was in love. Finally! She had fallen harder for Marcus than her sisters had for any of their boyfriends. She was sure about that.

"That's what happens to those who resist," Esther would mutter wisely.

So she wouldn't share the details of this evening with her sisters. Not ever. They were too precious and dear to her heart. Marcus's hesitancy, his slow finding of his way through the sorrows of his heart to break into the dawn of a new day. She would be his girlfriend. The best girlfriend Marcus could possibly have. Marcus had to see that now, clearly and plainly.

"*Goot* night," Mary chirped to several passing boys, headed towards the barn.

"*Goot* night," they replied, their gazes lingering on her, trying to figure out why she waited alone.

"Is someone getting your horse?" one of them paused to ask.

"Yep. Taken care of."

They laughed and moved on. Marcus met them coming out of the barn door. She couldn't hear what they said, but they were teasing him plenty. He was replying in kind, from the sound of their raucous voices. Marcus still had a smile on his face when he arrived, leading her horse with one hand and his with the other.

She took the bridle from him. "Yours first."

He nodded, his dreamy smile lingering.

She didn't ask what the teasing had been about. That was obvious. Her first date with Marcus being the center of the men's attention sent delightful shivers up and down her back.

Mary tied her horse to the hitching rack and helped Marcus hitch up. He did the same when they finished, and her horse was soon fastened between the shafts. He held the bridle while she climbed in.

"Be right after you," he said, letting go.

Mary held back on the reins, keeping her horse to a walk until Marcus's buggy caught up. She let go then, and their pace picked up, the sound of the horses' hooves pounding on the pavement like a drumbeat, with the moon now shedding its light on their path. Mary pinched herself. She simply couldn't believe this was happening.

When they arrived at the Hochstetlers' lane, Marcus slowed down to let Mary park first. Mary stopped short of the barn and hopped out to stand there waiting while he drove in and tied his horse to the hitching post. This felt more and more like an official date. His mouth was dry again as he walked towards where Mary had begun to unhitch her horse. He was dating the woman. The thought left him weak. He shook his head to clear it before he reached Mary. She already had her horse out of the shafts when he arrived.

"Which stall?" he asked, reaching for the bridle.

"I'll come with you," she said, and brought a flashlight out from under her buggy seat. He had forgotten his own. He was losing his mind. To cover his confusion, he clucked to the horse and led the way forward.

She opened the barn door, and the horse was soon in his stall, with a generous scoop of oats dumped in his bucket. They left him munching happily.

"Can we sit on the porch again?" Mary asked, the soft glow of the moonlight on her face. "I really don't have anything inside to eat."

"The porch is fine," he said, and followed her up the steps.

"I should tell Lavina we're here," Mary said, and vanished into the house.

He seated himself, the chains squawking above him.

She was back in a moment, carrying a blanket. "In case it gets chilly."

He took the side she offered him, brushing her fingers. Her presence was a comfort he had never imagined could grip his soul.

"It's lovely out here," she said, her hand finding his again.

"It is," he agreed as they swung slowly in the moonlight.

CHAPTER 25

Mary waited beside the buggy at the Hochstetlers' home two Sunday evenings later, while Marcus tied his horse to the hitching post. There were brownies and chocolate chip cookies in the cupboard. Both had been made fresh on Saturday. There was plenty of milk in the refrigerator. Leon had seen to that, eager to do his part to make the couple comfortable.

"That man's coming again," Leon had teased her while he was passing through the kitchen.

Lavina had shooed him on his way.

She was prepared tonight for her second date with Marcus. As usual, Marcus hadn't been in a rush. He had asked for another date in two weeks. She would gladly have agreed to one the following Sunday night, but they weren't dating steady yet, even if the community had long considered them a couple. She would have to accept that Marcus did things at his own pace.

Mary's gaze lingered on Marcus's broad shoulders as he pulled the blanket from the back of the buggy and carefully covered his horse. The moon was high in the sky, a half sliver compared to the glorious full moon which had celebrated their first date. The moon would be near the horizon by the time Marcus left at midnight. Two Sunday evenings ago they had sat on the porch swing under a blanket until eleven, simply enjoying each other's presence and the freshness of their status, getting used to the reality that they were finally together. For the last hour they had spent the time inside on the couch, playing checkers, which Marcus was good at, beating her three times in a row.

The next morning Leon had been full of teasing advice. "Don't feed him too much," he had warned, with a twinkle in his eye, "or kiss him more than once."

"Don't pay him mind," Lavina had told her.

Lavina had no objections to a display of affection between the two of them, but kissing took the consent of two people, and Marcus moved slowly.

"There!" Marcus proclaimed, the blanket finally secured. "That should keep him warm."

She moved closer and took his hand. "Come. I have brownies inside."

"That sounds delicious," he said.

"I would have had something the last time, but you gave me no warning."

"You do enough cooking for me during the week."

"But this calls for special food," she chided, and leaned against his shoulder.

She didn't dare show this kind of affection at the Yoders' house when Mose was around, but now it felt natural. She looked up into his face and squeezed his hand.

"We should sit on the porch swing again," he said, "but it's a little chilly."

"You're coming inside." She pulled on his hand, and he followed. She held the front door open for him and motioned towards the couch. "Wait until I bring the food."

He didn't object, settling down when she left.

"Hope you like these," she told him upon returning.

"You know I love your cooking." He took a brownie. "There is no doubt there."

She wanted to ask him if any doubt remained about their relationship, but didn't dare. He seemed to have fully made up his mind. Nothing that she had seen in the past weeks, either at the schoolhouse when Marcus stopped by or at the Yoders' home on the evenings she cooked supper for the two men, gave an indication otherwise.

"How are my siblings doing in school?" he asked, changing the subject. "Since they moved out I feel like I hardly see them."

"*Goot*, as always."

"I miss them," he said.

"Of course, but is it also a relief to know they're being well cared for elsewhere?"

"I suppose so," he said, sober-faced. "I think I've lumped together love and responsibility in my mind for a long time now. It feels weird to love them without having to take care of them, you know?"

"Makes perfect sense." Mary nodded, grateful that he could share that with her. "You should visit your mam more often."

"I should," he agreed. "In fact, Mam said the same thing this past Sunday. She invited me to join them on Saturday evenings for supper."

"Now nice!"

"I know." He laughed. "Between your cooking and Mam's, there is no chance I'll get thin."

"I will make certain of that." She offered him another brownie. "There are chocolate chip cookies in the cupboard."

"Have you decided about Christmas?" he asked, an unusual urgency in his voice.

"Ah . . . not really. With us dating, I don't feel like leaving, but on the other hand, my family will be offended if I don't come home."

"You aren't ready to get rid of me yet?"

She slapped his arm. "Don't even tease me on that subject. Why don't you come with me? That way I don't have to make a difficult decision."

"Are you ready for that?"

"For what? For letting people know that you are my boy-friend? I already wrote and told Mam."

"But seeing is believing."

"I don't have doubts, if that's what you mean."

"Neither do I," he said. "I should come along."

Silence settled around them for a moment. "We've come a long way, you know," she whispered.

"I was a fool that first day," he said. "I'm sorry about that."

"And I was rude and ungrateful," she said somberly. Then, after a moment of silence, "I'm using my shimmering luggage for the trip home."

He grinned. "You're not going to make this easy for me."

"No, because that's who I am."

He nodded. "That's who I fell in love with, turquoise blue suitcase and all."

She wanted to throw her arms around his neck and kiss him a thousand times for saying that, but instead she sat on the couch with her hands tightly clasped. "So you would really come?"

"Why not?"

"I want you to come. I did ask."

"Will your family like me?"

"They will love you. My sisters will trip over themselves admiring you. I can hear them gushing now."

He appeared quite interested. "Things like what?"

"How handsome you are. How manly and mature. They will think I did well."

"Your sisters would say that?"

"Believe me, they would."

"But I'm not handsome."

Mary gave him a baleful stare. "Don't kid yourself."

"At least you must think so. That's a comfort."

She wanted to hug him again, and run her hand over his freshly shaven chin, which would soon be sprouting a full-length beard if she had anything to say about things. She had tradition on her side. Amish men were required to wear a beard once they said their wedding vows.

"To a happy Christmas journey then." Marcus swallowed the last of his brownie, and washed it down with a long swig of milk.

"I'll write a letter tomorrow and tell Mam we are coming."

"And I'll find someone to help Mose with the chores while I'm gone."

"Are you ready for chocolate chip cookies?"

"Maybe later." Marcus settled back into the couch.

Mary gathered up the plate and empty glasses. "I'll be right back."

He nodded, lost in thought, apparently thinking about the trip to her community. "You will make a great impression," she assured him.

He smiled, his concentration unbroken.

Mary left him to his thoughts.

Marcus sat on the couch, listening to the clinking of plates in the kitchen. Mary would be back in a moment, but he was still thinking about the trip to her home community. Something niggled at him, but he couldn't pin down the thought. If Mary took him along, she was obviously serious about the relationship. He knew that already, so hesitation on Mary's part was not the problem. Once they arrived there would be plenty of questions asked about him. Mary was deeply loved in her home community, and everyone would want to know what his reputation was. He didn't expect any problems. Mary didn't have any boyfriends from former relationships, so there would be no disgruntled objections from jilted lovers. Something else bothered him though, and he figured it out about the time Mary returned and took her seat beside him on the couch.

"We should take care of something before we make the trip," he said.

Her face fell.

"No, nothing like that." He took her hand tenderly in both of his.

"What is it then?" She managed to smile.

"I'm not bringing up any doubts that I have, unless you object to what I am going to ask you. That would be bad."

"You're scaring me."

"Don't be scared," he said. "I think you should have something more to tell your parents and anyone else who asks about me than that you are dating me."

She stared at him. "Okay. I'm waiting."

"I would like to see you each Sunday evening from now on."

"So I could tell them that you are my steady?"

"If you want to be?"

"I would love that," she said, appearing pale.

"You would?"

"Of course. Why do you have to question?"

"I don't want to rush things."

She looked ready to wrap her arms around his neck.

"You aren't rushing things," she said. "But I am willing to wait."

For what? he almost asked, but he knew the answer. A quick look in her eyes told him that much. He had not been fair with Mary, making her wait so long for a proper date when, by all appearances to the rest of the community, they'd been a couple for months. She was different from him, exuberant and outgoing, and impulsive. He had been selfish to expect her to wait, and yet she had done so with patience and grace.

Her fingers moved in his hand. "I am so proud of you," she said. "How well you are handling the changes in your life—your mam's marriage, the farm thrown on your shoulders, the loss of your family—so quickly."

"They haven't gone too far," he said.

She ignored the objection. "You are a great man. You bore a heavy burden in your youth, and it didn't break you. Your heart was wounded, but you were willing to open that wound and find total healing." She gave a little laugh. "And you were open to me, the biggest upset you could have imagined."

"Mary." He tried to stop her. "Don't say those things."

"I will say them." A glint filled her eyes. "I will say them because they are true, and someone must say them. I will always admire you, as I have never admired a man. You have given me the answer to my dreams, when I hadn't even dreamed them."

A great well of emotion rose up inside of him, for this woman, this strange and wonderful creature who had brought such joy to his life. He loved her as he had never loved anything in life. He wanted to show her how much she meant to him, how her words healed the deep crevices of his heart that still ached from the loss of his father. She was like healing waters on a hot summer day, when strength returned to the body and even the soul seemed to right itself.

Her lips were still moving, but he didn't hear anything. He saw only her, and a deep thankfulness filled his heart. A desire stirred inside of him, a desire which followed his thankful heart, as naturally as the moon followed the setting of the sun, as if things had always been this way.

He reached for her, his fingers gentle on her face. She moved towards him on the couch, melting into his arms.

"Marcus," she whispered.

He silenced her with his lips on her mouth, and kissed her again and again.

EPILOGUE

LESS THAN A YEAR LATER, MARY STOOD IN FRONT OF THE BEDROOM mirror in her parents' old farmhouse with the flickering light of two kerosene lamps on the dresser beside her. Esther was placing the last pin into the belt of her wedding dress, and Lois was fussing with a string of loose hair falling out from beneath her white head covering.

Phoebe was fluttering about, viewing the progress from various angles.

"It's *goot* enough," Mary muttered to the three of them.

Her sisters ignored her.

"There," Esther declared, and stepped back to evaluate the dress. "Marcus will be much impressed."

"He's already impressed," Lois giggled. "I still can't believe our little sister has found such a besotted husband."

"You know it was bound to happen," Phoebe said. "The youngest are the prettiest and fall the hardest."

"Would you all be quiet?" Mary snapped. "The Lord led us and changed both of our hearts, and that's that."

"Just listen to her talk," Esther said, as if Mary wasn't in the room. "All our handsome men here in the community, and she has to travel somewhere else to find someone better."

"She *got* something better," Lois said. "You have to agree to that."

"I admit that reluctantly," Phoebe said.

"Stop it," Mary ordered.

They ignored her.

Esther was glaring at Phoebe. "You seemed quite impressed last Christmas when Mary showed up with Marcus in tow. Not much reluctance that I could see."

"Well, I had to admit the obvious," Phoebe said.

"He is quite handsome," Lois added.

"Are we done here?" Mary waved with both hands. "I have had enough. I can't breathe."

She rushed over to the window and undid the latch to push the frame upward. A warm breeze drifted inside, with a distant smell of fallen leaves and fresh-blown ground. The Lord had given her a glorious, sunny day for her wedding, as if to press home the point that His blessing truly was granted to her union with Marcus as husband and wife.

"Just look at her," Phoebe muttered. "Was I that lost in love?"

"Pretty much," Esther said. "I guess we all were."

"And still are," Lois said quietly.

Mary turned from the window and opened her arms. "My dear sisters, even though I had to run away from you to get married, I'm back, and I couldn't live without you."

"Then why are you moving to southern Ohio after the wedding?" Esther asked.

"Because that's where my husband lives," Mary said, tasting the word in her mouth. "My husband, or rather, soon to be husband."

"By twelve o'clock or so," Lois said. "Sure you don't want to change your mind?"

Mary slapped her playfully on the arm. "Thank you, all three of you, for helping me this morning, and for the work you have done on the wedding, and for . . ." Tears stung her eyes. "For being my sisters."

"Ah, she does love us," Esther said, taking Mary in her arms. "Our dear, dear little sister. How the Lord has blessed you with a *wunderbah* husband. We wouldn't want it any other way, and even when you live far, far away, you must come to visit, and we will visit you."

"Don't make it sound so dramatic." Mary wiped away the tears. "I'll only be a few hours south."

"What trash heap is this new husband of yours going to make you live in?" Lois asked playfully.

"Enough," Mary almost shouted. "Marcus lives on his deceased dat's farm, and it's no trash heap."

"Just checking," Phoebe said. "It's the handsome ones who pull the wool over your eyes."

"Are you speaking for yourself?" Mary shot back.

Phoebe laughed and gave Mary a hug. "I'll be down myself before long, maybe spring. Albert thinks we could make the trip after the planting. We'll see the place for ourselves, and this community that stole our little sister."

Lois was the last one to give Mary a hug, and held her the longest. "May the Lord's richest blessings be on you, little one. I couldn't have chosen a better husband for you if I had looked through a dozen communities."

"I thought so." Mary sniffled and searched for a handkerchief in the drawer. "I'll have my wedding dress soiled before too long."

Esther sprang into action, waving her hand about to dry any errant tears and searching for splatters on the dress.

"I was joking," Mary muttered. "I am being careful."

Her sisters ignored her, doing a final inspection before they left the room.

"You look perfect," Phoebe declared. "I guess we should have done our hugging before dressing the bride."

"Like such things can be scheduled." Lois held open the bedroom door. "Shall we go?"

Her three sisters also had tears in their eyes, even though they hid them well. Mary followed Lois out into the hall and down the stairs. Mam was in the kitchen when they arrived, and flanked by the threesome, she was presented with a flourish.

"Our bride of the day," Phoebe said, doing a fake bow.

Everyone laughed, but Mam was crying at the same time. "Here I thought this day would never come, but the Lord has had mercy upon an old woman. I shall die with all my daughters married to decent husbands."

"You are making a scene," Esther said. "Don't be so dramatic. This was inevitable."

Mary ignored them to hug Mam, and they wept on each other's shoulders. Her wedding dress would have tears stains, but they would dry by the time Marcus arrived from the place he was staying down the road. Tonight she would be with him as his wife. Mary let go of Mam, and Phoebe was already fanning her shoulder, while Esther sopped the wet spot with a Kleenex. She would be married today. There was nothing like actually arriving at your wedding day. Anticipation was one thing, but this was the day.

"Stop crying," Phoebe ordered. "No more tears."

Mam wiped her eyes. "I'm sorry. I was a little overcome."

"I love you, Mam," Mary whispered.

"Stop it," all three of her sisters ordered together. "Both of you can cry at the ceremony, not now."

But they wouldn't, Mary knew. There would be only happiness in a few hours when she said the sacred wedding vows with Marcus Yoder.

Marcus sat on the straight-back chair in the old pole barn, its rafters swept clean of spiderwebs and any fleck of dirt that he could see. The Wagler family had pulled out every stop in the wedding preparations for their youngest daughter.

A few familiar faces surrounded him as Bishop Mullet from his home community wound down the closing sermon. Mary had agreed at once when he suggested they ask Bishop Mullet to make the trip up from southern Ohio and perform the ceremony.

Mam was seated in the women's section, glowing with happiness. His siblings were in the crowd somewhere out of his sight, but they were here. Mary was in front of him, with her two attendants, wearing a light blue wedding dress. He hadn't been able to keep his eyes off of her since this morning when he arrived at the Wagler home, just as the sun was coming up over the horizon. The world had seemed to rejoice with him, cheering him onward in the new life he would begin with Mary by his side.

Mary had been in the house surrounded by her three sisters, who looked suspiciously at him, even though they were smiling. But everyone in this community had welcomed him with open arms when Mary brought him home last year for the Christmas holidays. He almost wished they were planning to live here after the wedding, instead of the farm in southern Ohio. But he belonged in his home community, and Mary had become a part of the place after one year of teaching. She had charmed everyone's hearts, and his most of all.

Marcus forced himself to focus on Bishop Mullet's preaching. He hadn't heard a word yet, and had absorbed little of the opening sermon with his attention completely captured by Mary's beauty.

"Marriage is of the Lord," Bishop Mullet was saying in his usual slow, thoughtful manner. "Though the sands of time have crept along for a thousand years, the Word of the Lord remains, one man and one woman who love each other, and are joined together hand in hand to walk through life as one. This is the beauty of what the Lord has done. We cannot, and will not, improve upon the work of the Lord. There are some who are asked to walk through life alone, but even they have the community to support them. Most of us are given the great gift of a partner to love and to honor, and to hold with all of our heart."

Bishop Mullet turned his attention from the congregation to look straight at Marcus and Mary. "If this couple still wishes to join their lives together in holy matrimony, the time has come to say the vows, so let them stand as a witness to their hearts' wish."

Marcus felt like leaping to his feet, but he stood slowly, and Mary was doing likewise, following his lead. Mary stepped across the distance between them into a stream of light that was playing across the hardwood floor. The lower part of her dress was caught in the brilliance and shimmered brightly as Mary stood by his side in front of Bishop Mullet.

Marcus couldn't keep a smile off his face as he lifted his gaze to answer Bishop Mullet's first question.

"Do you believe, Brother Marcus Yoder, that the Lord has given you this sister, Mary Wagler, to you, as your lawful wedded wife?"

"Yah," he said firmly.

Mary said yah to her question, and Bishop Mullet continued.

When the bishop finished, he reached for their hands and placed them together, "I join you," he said, "in the name of the God of Abraham, Isaac, and Jacob, as husband and wife. What God joined together, let no man tear apart."

Mary was smiling up at him. She wanted him to kiss her in front of everyone, but Amish men didn't kiss their wives in public.

His wife, he thought. Mary was his wife. He let go of her hand and they seated themselves again. The last song number was given out, and the singing began. He snuck a glance at Mary, who was still smiling, the lower corner of her dress caught in the ray of sunlight. She had never looked more beautiful to him.